Crossings 34

Home

© 2022, Kossi A. Komla-Ebri
© 2022, Translation by Marie Orton

Library of Congress Cataloging-in-Publication Data

Names: Komla-Ebri, Kossi, author. | Orton, Marie, 1965- translator.
Title: Home / Kossi A. Komla-Ebri ; translated by Marie Orton.
Description: New York, NY : Bordighera Press, [2022] | Series: Crossings ; 34
    | Summary: "Home finds Kossi Komla-Ebri between places and identities,
    cultures and languages, expectations and realities, Europe and Africa. Across
    these eleven short stories, Komla-Ebri crosses genres and borders with an
    expansiveness that welcomes readers into an ever increasing interconnected
    world and all the struggles that come with it"-- Provided by publisher.
Identifiers: LCCN 2022019392 | ISBN 9781599541907 (trade paperback)
Subjects: LCSH: Komla-Ebri, Kossi--Translations into English. | LCGFT: Short
    stories.
Classification: LCC PQ4911.O55 H66 2022 | DDC 853/.92--dc23/eng/20220426
LC record available at https://lccn.loc.gov/2022019392

Printed by Ingram Lightning Source.

Published by
BORDIGHERA PRESS
John D. Calandra Italian American Institute
25 W. 43rd Street, 17th Floor
New York, NY 10036

Crossings 34
ISBN 978-1-59954-190-7

HOME

Kossi A. Komla-Ebri

Translated by Marie Orton

BORDIGHERA PRESS

TABLE OF CONTENTS

GOING HOME

Heaven may not know it
But the earth is covered with footsteps,
The reluctant footsteps of those who leave
To seek a home.
For home is not only
Here where you were born,
But it is where
The man that is in you
Can look up at the sky at last, grateful
For the day that ends
And can hope
In the day that will come

DONATELLA MARTELLI AVANZI

"Yao, if you want to go back to Abidjan,[1] I have a plane ticket for you on tomorrow's flight."

This was his brother-in-law's idea.

"Really?" Yao asked incredulously.

"Yes! But . . ."

It was a Sunday afternoon, a beautiful spring day. After greeting the African girls from his sister's boarding school, Yao headed home. Getting on the metro at the Montrouge station, he walked, almost skipping, trying to suppress the anxious tumultuous joy that was trying to escape from the tips of his toes up through the roots of his hair and out his eyes. He couldn't repress the quiver in his soul that

---

1 The capital of Ivory Coast.

had turned into a tension so intense it made his muscles ache. He tried to take deep breaths, tried to order his thoughts, but he couldn't hold back that deafening cry echoing deep inside. After hopping the turnstile to dodge paying the ticket, he continued jubilantly down the endless metro tunnel in the direction of Porte de Clignancourt, fists clenched, waving his arms in triumph, and finally burst out, with his arms outstretched and all the strength he could give to his voice: "I'm going hoooomme!!!"

In the half-light of the empty tunnel, an echo returned with an almost ironic "Oh . . ." But in his sparkling happiness, Yao paid no attention.

He swayed on his feet, immersed in his thoughts, turning a blind eye to the crowd of passengers pushing him into the old subway car with its hard wooden benches.

One thought expanded in his mind until it occupied it entirely: "I'm going home, I won't get up at dawn every morning and drag myself like a zombie through the metro, the RER,[2] then buses, and then walk miles to get to the Halles of Rungis in the hopes of finding some fruit and vegetable trucks to unload, and then stand freezing in cold storage. No sir, never again will I have to drag myself back in the evening with a shattered spine just to stretch out on a cramped bed in that cramped room in Rue Barbes, while I listen to my stomach rumbling from hunger."

Who would have thought that life in Paris would be so inhumane?

After all his years here, Yao was still amazed at the love-hate relationship he had with the city.

Of course, Paris was beautiful, this was an irrefutable truth.

Paris could enchant you, from the wandering Seine to the cobblestones of Notre Dame, not to mention the Luxembourg gardens. The Latin Quarter was fascinating with its fire-eaters, acrobats, bookstores, and *caveaux*.[3] Just sitting there at the Archangel's fountain gave you a sense of freedom. It was pleasant there early in the morning to go from Blanche to Montmartre's imposing cathedral, then wander

---

2   *Réseau Express Régional* [Regional Express Network]: Paris' system of suburban commuter trains and rapid transit trains.

3   Cellars.

around the Place du Tertre when things weren't cordoned off, parceled off, and organized coldly.

It was actually delightful to stroll around with one's hands in one's pockets sniffing the pungent air, to walk with a bohemian step, to browse among the masters of copying, the chiselers of profiles, the skilled draftsmen and the geniuses of the pencil who in a few minutes immortalized portraits, under the astonished and admiring eyes of the tourists. Yao, with his restless soul, couldn't help but fall in love with the Paris of postcards, the Paris of the bistros, of *panaché*,[4] the Eiffel Tower, *pommes frites*, oysters, and the luminous and luxurious sensuality of the Champs Elysées.

Living in Rue Barbes, how many times had the torrid and unconfessable desires of lust dragged him, painfully, to beg and peek with lowered, furtive and ashamed eyes at the daring photos in sex stores, from the Tati store of Pigalle to Blanche.

And yes, he hated Paris, because it knew how to be cruel and demanding like his beloved who only deigned to gratify him for the feel of money: the Paris of multicolored Arab sweets, of giant pictures of spaghetti Bolognese and steak-frites, making him salivate while his cramped guts twisted in hunger; he could fill his eyes but was forced to turn home, satiated only in his imagination, to drink water heavy with the stench of chlorine because he was penniless. He hated that cynical city, which when you were too far from the city's famous public urinals wouldn't even let you use the bathroom in a bar because you didn't have a franc.

The abrupt braking of the metro brought him back to reality: he had arrived at his destination—surely for the last time!

Leaving the metro, he was swallowed up by the motley throng of poor people pressing through the entrance to the Tati store. There, the

---

4   A drink mixing beer and soda.

flimsy and outdated, bright-colored clothes were sold cheaply and, in the confusion, with a bit of luck and some cunning, it was easy enough to slip a pair of socks or underwear into your pocket.

Today Yao was too happy to go "shopping." Turning the corner of the street, he didn't even stop to chat with his blonde friend Annie, who teetered unsteadily on the clattering high heels of her black ankle boots as she walked up and down the adjacent narrow street where she would liberally open her black jacket to expose her brimming merchandise to the porcine eyes of possible customers while crooning in her husky voice, "Alors, Chéri, tu viens?"[5]

"Hello Yao!" murmured the girl when she saw him.

Yao returned her greeting with a wave of his hand and a complicit smile. He crossed the threshold of his building with no elevator where he lived in the attic.

As he climbed the stairs, he thought of Annie and her companions for whom he felt a great regard. Chatting with the girls many times, he had discovered how loyal and supportive they could be of each other and of people who, like him, had to live by their wits in the winding tracks of the rough and stingy City of Lights. These days, public opinion and the media herded drug addicts, prostitutes, gays, delinquents, immigrants, and sometimes even the handicapped into a single pen located on the borders of respectability and did it the courtesy of the most hypocritical forms of legality.

Yao remembered that on his way home a few months earlier, it was Annie who stopped him, "Yao! Watch out, there have been *flics*."[6] He spun around bewildered like a hunted animal, as he felt his legs go weak and his heart throbbing in his throat. But he replied in a tone that wished it could swagger, "You've got to be kidding!"

Yao realized with astonishment that the girl had called him by his own name, and not by his street name, "Eric," the name he hid behind as a precaution for his more or less illicit activities. A thought came to his mind, quick as lightening and convinced him danger was imminent.

---

5   "Are you coming, sweetheart?"

6   Police.

"The *flics* came. They caught your cousin at Dudu's with the goods. They poked around at your place and questioned us about you."

"That's how she knew my real name," Yao thought before running off. He roamed around Paris all night, looking over his shoulder, wandering and changing directions a thousand times. Then finally exhausted, he stopped to think. It was certainly pointless to run away; if the police were looking for him, sooner or later they would find him. He might as well give up now and face it. Resigned, he took the subway and returned home calmly and resolutely.

At home, he found the door open and an incredible mess in the room. His suitcase was still there, open, with his things scattered about. With a sigh of relief, he saw that his passport and all his documents were there. He walked over to the skylight and stretched his hand out in search of the lanyard attached to the bag containing the stockpile of goods. The plastic bag was gone. The envelope at the bottom of the suitcase with his last remaining loose change was there, intact, proof that this had not been the work of thieves. He sat on the bed waiting for the cops to arrive, convinced that they were there somewhere waiting for him.

Two hours passed, then four, but no one came. The arrangement with his cousin must have worked like a charm. They had agreed, "If one of us gets caught, then he will cover for the other; that way, one of us will be free to get the first one out of prison." Back then, still full of illusions, his cousin had further coached him, "Just say you're here visiting me, and you don't know anything about what I do, and I'll say the same. The police don't beat people here anyway like they do at home, and for a few grams they'll keep me in jail for a week at the most."

Actually, they beat him thoroughly with an iron rod across the soles of his feet and left him in jail for four months.

As Yao walked up the stairs and thought back on all this, he was happy that he could finally escape it all. By now he'd found a lawyer for his cousin and arranged to cover the expenses. He was afraid now and seeing his cousin behind bars had stripped him of his illusions, so this plane ticket for home was a boon falling from the sky. He'd had enough of this adventure in the Whites' country; Yao wanted to go home.

The arrest of his cousin felt like an omen, directing him back to the right path. Going home was his long-awaited chance to escape the trap of drugs.

He lay down unable to fall asleep. The excitement of returning to Ivory Coast tomorrow was too great. He was leaving this cold country with its cold climate and, above all, its cold people.

He was going home, yes, home to his country where no one would ever refuse to serve him in a bar. In Paris he'd tried everything: he'd tried sleeping ten to a frigid room, taking turns sleeping on the hard floor and the rickety sofa, where five people sat with their feet up on the chairs, huddling together to shelter from the north wind that filtered through the window frames and stung their bones, howling around the edges of the piece of cardboard that substituted for glass in the door. Just thinking about it gave him goosebumps. It seemed to him that he could still smell that mixed stench of rancid, musty, and spicy odors that he invariably carried with him, despite his frequent ablutions in the public showers. Yes, sir, he was going home: he would never ever again rummage through the trash bins at night behind the supermarkets to feed himself, much less duck into the metro pretending to tie his shoes so he could pick up cigarette butts.

"Girls!" He'd announced strutting haughtily, waving his ticket at the African schoolgirls. "Girls, while you'll still be here suffering from the cold, think of me roasting in the heat tomorrow!" Then seeing their dreamy and nostalgic looks, he added wickedly and mercilessly: "Girls, I'll spare you the descriptions of spicy kebabs, *attieké*,[7] peanut sauce, and *fufu*;[8] I won't mention the intoxicating nights, dancing until dawn to the rhythm of reggae, coupé décalé, soukous, zaiko, and merengue, as I'm squeezed tight by real African girls, not white girls dyed black like you, warm African girls with their firm, beautiful breasts." On his way out, Yao concluded his

---

7   A fermented cassava dish.

8   A West African dish made from mashed yams, cassava roots, and/or plantains.

little show with a James Brown twist, exclaiming: "So long, girls! I'll say hello to Africa for you!"

Yao spent the night evaluating the past and dreaming of the future, an uncertain future, but one that could not be worse than the present. In the morning, he quickly gathered his few belongings and put them in his suitcase.

He picked up his guitar, greeted the concierge who had always been very motherly to him, and handed her the keys. For the first time, she kissed him and murmured, "Say hello to your mom for me!" as if she'd known his mother for years with how often Yao had mentioned her.

"I will, I promise."

Yao didn't have enough money to take a cab to the airport, so he took the metro to the nearest stop in the direction of the airport. He'd hitchhike from there. The plane was leaving in the afternoon and he'd have plenty of time. He arrived at the subway entrance. Luck was on his side: the conductor's office was empty. He hopped the turnstile and dragged his luggage along.

At the end of the line, Yao counted the change remaining in his pocket. It wasn't enough for the bus. He got on without paying, despite the driver's accusing stare in the mirror. He sat in the front seat so he could skip out at the first sign of a ticket inspector, and his precaution paid off, because at the fifth stop Yao spotted them. The officials stopped him just as he got off.

"Ticket, please."

"I don't have one."

"ID and address, then."

Without arguing, Yao gave them an address he kept for just such occasions; it was written on an envelope that he'd pasted a cancelled stamp onto, all while he thought, "I'm going home anyway!"

He walked along the road for a while, but his heavy suitcase was beginning to dig into the palm of his hand.

After a kilometer, he stopped and sat on his luggage, tried to hitchhike, but no one stopped. He still had plenty of time ahead of him, but the agonizing thought of missing the plane tugged at his mind.

He then decided to do something he'd never done in his life: beg. He'd always felt ashamed to ask for money and had even frowned upon the beggars who tried to stop him in the tunnels of the metro. Now he finally understood. He knew that when a man feels like a cornered animal, then morality becomes a luxury, irrelevant to survival, like wearing a flower in a buttonhole. To overcome his own embarrassment, he thought of asking the person's address when borrowing the money, so as to return it as soon as he got home.

Before he could approach a girl he saw walking up the street, she either sensed or misunderstood his intentions and hastily crossed the road to the other side.

He then approached an elderly woman, but as soon as he opened his mouth, she started in fear, clutched her purse to her chest, letting out a sharp cry. She hurried around Yao but continued to peer suspiciously behind her even several meters on.

These first two attempts convinced Yao not to approach women.

He turned to a man clutching a baguette under his sweaty armpits: "Can you please lend me five francs?"

The man walked past not even dignifying Yao with a glance, though he could be heard muttering "Go home" under his breath.

Yao felt himself seething with anger, but even more with shame, still he continued to ask now with his eyes downcast, not daring to look anyone in the eye. It seemed that all the people on the street were watching him and he read in their eyes and in their minds the same judgment, "You good-for-nothing *nègre*, get a job. Better yet, why don't you just go home?"

Yao was humiliated and disheartened, he believed this behavior shamed all of his race.

He remembered one evening when, driven by hunger, with his groaning belly burning, as he was rummaging around in a trash can, he was surprised by a girl, "What are you doing?"

"Can't you tell?" he replied defensively.

"Are you hungry?"

"What kind of question is that?"

"Do you want to come eat at my house?"

Yao looked at her in disbelief and distrust, wondering what the catch was, but driven by desperation he agreed.

The girl took him to dinner with her parents. They were polite, talking about Africa and music. At the table, he ate his fill. No one asked him what country he was from, what he did, or even his name with that police-style tone of interrogation that people usually used to grill foreigners on the pretext of getting to know them.

As he remembered the episode, Yao relentlessly continued his quest back home.

He almost repeated his plea to a young man before registering his appearance, his clothing. He was wearing a pair of ragged, washed-out jeans, had long hair, and a tattoo on his wrist. Yao was about to pull his hand back when the young man took out his wallet, handed him two ten franc bills, and promptly disappeared.

Yao stood there for a moment in astonishment, regretting having judged a man's heart by his outward appearance. Moved, he promised himself that he would never, ever refuse to give money or help to anyone who asked from now on. Sure, he knew of people who exploited other people's pity, but today he understood some who begged really were in trouble. Yes, he would pay this help forward.

He arrived at the airport on time. Yao had time to treat himself to a sandwich and a beer before going to check in. A tremor of dull anguish rippled over his heart.

When he'd offered Yao the plane ticket, his brother-in-law had explained, "It's the return ticket tied to my scholarship. My name is written on it, but don't worry, no one will ask for your ID when you check in, it's just an African name to them. Don't worry, everything will be fine. Just as a precaution, I'll give you my passport, because White people think we Blacks all look alike, so they won't know the difference. Don't worry!" Thus reassured, Yao was so happy about the chance to go home that he didn't consider that between saying something and actually doing it, there was not just "a sea of difference," as the old Italian saying went, but there was also a long line and a long wait, full of anxiety. But Yao could tell that the spirits of the ancestors were with him, because when he reached the counter, a young lady with a radiant smile checked his suitcase, reserved a smoking seat for him, and advised him to keep his guitar with him so as not to risk breaking it. Yao gave her one of his wide *charmeur* smiles and took the liberty to comment gallantly: "Thank you! You are very kind as well as pretty!" Then he thought with a heart full of joy: "It's done! I'm going home!"

He walked lightly past the metal detectors and towards passport control. As he stood in line, he was seized by a doubt: "Is it better to show my own passport or my brother-in-law's?

In the end he decided to show his brother-in-law's passport, because "for White people, all Blacks look alike," plus you never know if the name on the passport is connected with the passenger manifest.

Yao raised his head and his heart stopped beating for an interminable second. At the head of his line, checking passports, was a black policeman from the French islands.

"Damn!" he thought, "He'll know right away it's not me in the picture for sure!" He quickly changed lines and headed toward a plump, good-natured-looking white policeman. When his turn came, Yao inhaled the warm air into the top of his lungs to slow down the deafening beats of his heart, and handed over his brother-in-law's passport with an air of indifference and boredom. The policeman took the document and raised the stamp to validate it. His hand stopped in mid-air, he looked at the photo, then at Yao, who tried to flash a shy smile, then back at the photo again. Puzzled, brow furrowed, the chubby official suggested hesitantly, "But . . . this isn't you in the picture!"

For a moment, the blood froze in Yao's veins and everything spun around.

"Oh, yes, that's me!" he argued, tentatively.

"No! It's not you!" The policeman asserted more confidently and continued, "This person has a beard!"

"I shaved my beard," Yao declared, lying firmly through his teeth.

"No! That's not you on the picture!" declared the officer, staring him in the eyes.

"You're right," Yao admitted, stuttering, taking his passport from his pocket, on the verge of despair. "Let me explain," he whispered, as he bent towards the policeman so as not to be heard. "It's my brother-in-law's passport; he . . ."

"Come with me to the security office!" demanded the officer, getting up without heeding Yao's attempts to explain.

"Oh God! My God, how humiliating!" thought Yao as he followed the man, feeling the murmurs and the stares of the other travelers piercing the back of his neck. It was as if time and space were suddenly arrested, frozen in a vacuum of anguish. His head felt empty and his body grew heavy.

In the hallway on the way to the security office, the policeman coldly reiterated: "You can't travel with someone else's documents!"

"I know! But since I had my brother-in-law's ticket, we thought..."

Yao stopped talking because the man wasn't listening. He took another tack: "Do you think we could possibly come to some kind of agreement, I mean . . ."

He realized he'd better shut up, rather than make his situation worse with an attempt at bribery.

Yao bitterly regretted not staying in his original line. Surely his Black "brother" would have been more understanding and would have turned a blind eye to what Yao considered an unimportant detail.

At the security office, the officials immediately called him by his first name. Yao was searched and interrogated: "Whose passport did you steal and where did you get it?" "How do we know that the passport belongs to your brother-in-law? Your surnames are different." "Where did you steal the ticket?" "You'd better tell the truth, otherwise we'll lock you up!"

Yao had to repeat his story ten times, sweating, agitated, now standing, pacing the room with his hands in his pockets.

"Please! You have to believe me! Just let me go home." Then he grew angry and aggressive: "What does it matter to you? You can see that I have my passport in order. Why would I have used my brother-in-law's passport except for the ticket? On TV, in the papers, all you ever do is tell us to go back home, that you don't want to see us around. Do you really want to send us back or not? Well, now I want to leave, now that I want to go home, you're keeping me here! What's the point of that? Tell me, what's the point?"

Confronted with their impassive looks, Yao returned to an aggrieved tone: "Please, I'm begging you, let me go. I can't stay here, the hunger, the cold. If I go back to the city now, I won't have a place to stay, I don't have a job anymore. Please, just let me go back to my home!"

Through it all, Yao tried to suppress the rising tears of despair. He didn't want to cry in front of these men, he wanted to save a shred of his shattered dignity. His mouth was dry and his throat parched and sore, he fell silent. Tears he could not check ran down his cheeks to die silently at the corners of his dry lips. The chief constable picked up the phone and gestured for him to take a seat in the waiting room.

Yao called upon on all the saints and spirits of his ancestors.

Not five minutes later, a long lanky man in suit arrived wearing an Air France badge and a walkie-talkie clipped to his belt. He immediately lit into Yao, "This is a scam against our company, you cannot travel with someone else's ticket without our consent."

"What does it matter to you, the seat has already been paid for!"

"It matters, young man, it matters! It makes a difference as far as insurance is concerned. In case of an accident, you aren't officially among our passengers!"

Yao at that point gave up arguing. He could see that fate wanted it that way; even if he couldn't understand the reason today, someday it would be clear.

Resigned, he sat down on the sofa with his guitar in his lap.

He didn't know if it was his silence or his defeated face that softened the long lanky man, because Yao heard him fiddling with the walkie-talkie, talking a little, then turning to Yao, he said, "Come on! I'll take you to the plane, we still have time!"

Yao suddenly straightened up, euphoric, mentally thanking his guardian angel and the spirits of his ancestors, and followed the man towards the large, covered tube leading to the plane.

From a distance he saw the flight attendant standing in front of the still open door to the aircraft.

He made it just in time, "I'm going home!"

The echo of hurried footsteps sounded behind them.

The Air France agent turned around as the voice of the fat policeman called out, "Where are you taking him? Look, I've already made my report."

The airline agent stopped instantly, gently but firmly blocking Yao with his outstretched arm, keeping him from boarding.

"I'm sorry, but I can't risk my job for you."

They looked into each other's eyes for a moment. The agent assumed a distant gaze and a detached, professional attitude.

"Goodbye!" His handshake was warm.

Yao went back to sign the statement at the security office. He no longer felt anything. When the pain in the soul reaches its peak, the heart convulses, and nothing can be felt anymore. They let him go after a lecture that slid off the thick bark of his indifference. He picked up his guitar, went to request his suitcase.

"It's already been loaded," was the reply.

"At least my bag will be able to enjoy the African sun," he remarked ironically to the employee who looked at him without understanding.

Suddenly Yao felt an overwhelming fatigue invade his body.

He dragged himself and the weight of his sadness towards the bus stop. When the bus arrived, he searched his pockets for the remaining ten francs that the generous man had given him, but found only a handkerchief and a guitar pick. He hesitated for a moment with his foot on the step of the bus. The driver grumbled, "Well, what?"

Yao searched again for the ten-franc bill, rummaging in vain through every pocket he had: there was no trace of the money. He pulled his foot back. The driver angrily shifted into gear and drove off, and Yao stood there with his arms shaking, leaning on his guitar.

He turned to look at the ground: nothing. "The cops took my money!" he thought and began to laugh hysterically, shaken by an uncontrollable and liberating paroxysm.

After a while he stopped laughing and took stock of the situation coldly: "I thought I'd be home by now, but I'm still here. The only clothes I have are the ones I'm wearing, I don't have a franc in my pocket, but I still have fifteen days of rent already paid for my room in Rue Barbes and after all I'm still alive. I just have to find a way back to the city."

He made his decision. He took a cab.

Near the front door of Rue Barbes, he saw Annie.

"Hi, Yao!"

"Hi, Annie! Can you lend me money for the cab? I'm broke."

"Sure!" she nodded, opening her purse.

"Thank you, Annie, you're such a friend. You understand life is hard, but the important thing is to be alive. I'll survive despite the walls of words, laws, borders, and prejudices that men continue to erect to divide them, to make life impossible. I'll survive as long as there are people like you who care and can look beyond the limits of appearances."

She looked at him, eyes widening, "Yao, are you okay?"

"Yes. I'm fine in spite of everything . . . I'll explain . . . I'm going to sleep now."

He walked by the door to collect his keys. The landlady looked at him and didn't ask anything. She just said, "Welcome home, Yao."

"Thank you!" He replied with a disconsolate smile, thinking about the girls' faces at the boarding house when they would see him again.

WHEN I CROSS THE RIVER

"When memory hunts for wood to warm itself with nostalgia, it chooses only the best logs . . ."

It is true that "a man never returns to his mother's womb, but he gladly returns to his native village."

I remember when I was a young student in France returning home one summer to my village Hanyigba in Togo, that village of ours gripping the mountains.

We are mountain people, at least that's what they say about us, but the highest point of our mountain is barely nine hundred meters. It's quite true that "he who has never left home thinks only his mother can make good sauce."

One evening that summer there was a full moon, a moon so bright it lit up the starry sky as if it were broad daylight. A sky so close it seemed you could reach out and touch it with your hand and the wind brought the woven voices of the vodou ceremonial drums as if they were the vapors of a perfume.

Before saying good-night with his usual, "I'm going to bed, may God wake us up," that night my father said: "Tomorrow morning we must wake up early; we have a judgment in the Ablomé neighborhood."

Seeing my expression, he continued: "Yes, I know you are not yet old enough to sit with us, but the elders have decided that your level of study, and the fact that you have traveled, gives you the right to sit under the tree of *palabre*.[1] Go rest; tomorrow you will be with us in Ablomé."

My father re-entered his room before I began to realize the honor given to me.

---

1   From French, an expression to indicate the assembly place in regions across Africa where issues concerning the community are discussed.

I spent the night brooding, a thousand thoughts spinning in my mind: how should I behave, could I have the patience to deal with the numerous codified rituals of the *palabre*, especially since by now I had become accustomed to summarizing when I spoke, getting straight to the heart of the matter. (To tell the truth, to this day my wife still complains about my long-windedness and chattiness, but we know that "a log of wood even if it stays in the river for years will never become a crocodile.")

It seemed that I'd just fallen asleep when the gentle but firm hand of my father shook me awake. Oh, God! It was half past four in the morning! As was our custom, he woke me up without saying a word, because we do not speak without having first washed out our mouths. The mouth is the temple of the word and the word is sacred for us.

After rinsing out my mouth, I went to my father and presented my morning greeting to him, bowing at the middle with my right hand extended toward him and my left hand holding the elbow beneath my right forearm: "It is daylight."

And he replied: "It is daylight. Did you wake up?"

"Yes, thank you for yesterday."

"You're welcome."

It is customary to always thank people for their favors of the previous days because, in a society like ours where the rule of solidarity is the law, "the only one that allows us to survive," we are always indebted to someone for something.

After this brief greeting laced with silences, we walked towards Ablomé. Although it was dawn, multiple sounds mixed together along the paths that flanked the houses: the snoring behind open windows, the barking of the occasional dog, the hungry cries of some children, the first timid attempts of a few roosters, and the rustling of brooms made of palm branches used by the young girls already cleaning the courtyards. My father walked forward with his *kente* gathered around his waist and the surplus fabric thrown over his left shoulder (as the ancient Romans used to do), chewing on a bit of wood which we used to clean our teeth.

At that uncertain hour between night and day, the air still heavy with men's dreams, we walked at a good pace, stopping only to say

hello to those who were already headed to the fields to work; as well
as those who were going to the public toilets made of a tree trunk
tossed down near a ditch, naturally making conversation while seeing
to their physical needs. It was customary to greet everyone along the
way even if we did not know each other:

"It's daylight."

"It's getting light."

"Did you wake up?"

"And the children?" ("how are they"? even if you don't have any.)

"And your wife?"

"What about your husband?"

"And your father?"

"And work?"

As we passed each other, the greeting continued like an echo of
monkish litanies:

"Give my regards to those in the camp!"

"Give my regards to those in Ablomé!"

"Yes . . . and thank you for the favor yesterday."

"You're welcome."

And so it went on as long as a person was within earshot, then
another person would come past and it would start over again. Words
and greetings are sacred to us; not greeting each other is inconceivable,
such an act would be laden with meaning, a bad omen.

We arrived in Ablomé in the courtyard of old Nukuku. "Nukuku" in
my language means "dead thing," and in Europe one would immediately
react, "What an ugly name!" but actually it's a name for good luck,
because her parents had lost all their children in infancy that were born
before her. When she was born, her mother named her "Nukuku" to
keep her alive because by calling her "Dead Thing," her mother was
sure that death would not take the baby away. What would Death do
with a dead thing? Indeed, Death spared Dead Thing until she became
a grumpy old woman with a face furrowed by the snares of life.

Strength and power of the Word, the power of the Name. The
Word can therefore defeat death.

The courtyard of the elderly Nukuku was already crowded with
people and a chorus of "Welcome, you who have walked!" greeted

us as we crossed the threshold. We sat under the thatched roof in the courtyard with the elders and notables of the village in a semicircle facing Nukuku's house. They brought us water in a half gourd as a ritual sign of welcome and after pouring a few drops on the ground for the spirits of the ancestors as is the custom in our country (I think in Europe they raise a glass to take heaven as a witness), we drank a sip, not caring much about the water's color or its small guests.

I turned to look around. Without a doubt I was the youngest in the assembly. In the middle of the semicircle sat the village chief whom we all respectfully call Togbe, or "grandfather," not because he was old or the oldest there, but because he embodied wisdom. In our land, before the arrival of colonization with its culture of writing, there was only oral culture. History, knowledge, customs, traditions, social rules, all of it was handed down from mouth to ear, through the word, and therefore those who survived the longest were those who knew more and had more experience; the older they became, the wiser they became, because they were forged by the experiences of life. At that time, the village historians were the *griots*, our storytellers. In the evenings, the grandparents handed down the rules of society and the stories of the village through fables, parables, and riddles. The elders are the historical memory of our villages, and this is where the famous phrase of the Malian writer Amadou Hampâté Bâ comes from: "In Africa when an elder dies, a library has burned down."

In the middle of the semicircle, Togbe sat surrounded by his dignitaries, the notables, and the village elders. Some inhaled voluptuous puffs of smoke from their terra cotta pipes, others snuffed the powdered tobacco balanced on their thumbnail, then let out a big sneeze, still others chewed bits of cola with obvious satisfaction. Some looked at me, then looked at my father, and silently nodded their heads as lizards do. I heard a voice say, "The son of Fofoé is now a man!"

One of the dignitaries, Yawovi of Nukuku's family, raised his voice and said "Agoo!"[2] a couple of times.

Everyone stopped talking among themselves to direct their attention to him.

---

2   From Ewe, an expression meaning both "permission" as well as "silence."

"Agoo!"

Then crouching down and facing the village chief he said, "Togbe welcome," then to everyone, "Welcome."

To which one of the elders, Papa Wadefe, replied, "Togbe, our chief, lets you know that he is at peace and hopes that all of you are also at peace."

All assented in chorus.

"Togbe," resumed the elder Wadefe, "Togbe would like to know the reason for this morning summons. While it is true that what is sown early soon bears fruit, it is equally true that one does not light a fire if one has nothing to put on it. What do the elders of Nukuku's family tell us?"

A long silence followed in which everyone pondered on the wisdom and significance of the elder Wadefe, his knowledge of proverbs and the art of his speech. We say that "proverbs are the palm oil to make words join with ideas," and that "a proverb is the steed of the word: when the word is lost, with the help of the proverb, it is found again."

After that silence, the dignitary Yawovi took up the word again, addressing the elder Wadefe: "I beg Papa Wadefe to hear with his mind and heart these words of mine, and to convey them to our leader in such a way that they may reach the hearts and minds of all present here. Everyone present here knows that we are together in the elderly Nukuku's courtyard. My cousin Nukuku, as you all know, is seriously ill and has been bedridden for a fortnight in one of the huts here in front of us: her hours are now numbered and she is preparing to take the path that leads to the great river . . ."

It is a belief among us that life and death are on opposite sides of the same river, and to die is nothing more than to cross the river.

"Yesterday," resumed Yawovi, "her daughter Abra, who has been living in the city for years now, came seeking our help. Years ago, after a furious argument with her mother, before Abra left home forever, her mother told her these exact words: 'Do what you will, my daughter, but as sure as my name is Nukuku, when I cross the river . . . you will cross the river with me.'"

At such grave words, a chill shook the whole assembly into an icy silence. Then Yawovi continued explaining that, with her mother now on the path to the river, Abra had begun to feel sick in the city, to feel a burning inside her every day, sometimes in her belly, then in her legs, then in her hips. All over her body, she felt like ants were running under her skin or an electric current was running under her hair. The white doctors in town didn't understand and gave her drops that only made her sleep.

Finally, Abra, exhausted, had gone to consult a soothsayer who had told her while looking at the shells, "Sometimes it is difficult to separate the fingernail from the finger, the pestle from the mortar . . . go back to your village and you will understand . . ."

Abra returned to find her mother in agony, to remember her mother's dreadful statement: "When I cross the river . . . you will cross the river with me," to understand the strength and power of the Word. The Word that can defeat death. Can the Word that defeats death also bring death?

The family council was immediately summoned and went to the old woman's bedside to ask her to withdraw her words so as not to add misfortune upon misfortune.

But she answered their pleas with silence.

"That is why we woke you up this morning to ask for your opinion: it is known that the river makes detours because there is no one to show it the right way. And here my voice falls," concluded Yawovi.

After a long silence, Papa Wadefe turned to the village chief and said: "Togbe, have your son's words reached you?"

He nodded, then turned to the rest and asked: "Assembly, have you heard the words of Yawovi?" and all assented.

Papa Wadefe, turning his head towards the village chief, then said, "Togbe, hear my words and may they be carried on the wings of the wind to the heart of Yawovi. Tell him that the council of elders is honored by his trust, but just as you cannot ask a blind man to recognize white from black, you cannot ask us for judgment without telling us in truth what happened between Nukuku and her daughter that brought the mother to the point of pronouncing such a serious sentence."

Togbe turned to Yawovi: "Did you hear that?"

Yawovi replied, "Togbe, be my messenger to Papa Wadefe and the whole assembly; all of us here are familiar with the story of Nukuku and Abra. We all know how ill-tempered Nukuku became when her husband ran off with the foreign woman and how demanding Nukuku was of her daughter from the time she was a young girl, how she made the girl clean the courtyard a thousand times because it was never tidy enough for her. The sauce her daughter made was never to her taste; sometimes it was too salty or not salty enough, other times it was too spicy or not spicy enough. All of us here remember when Abra came of age to choose a man for her life, of those who asked for her hand, not one was considered worthy of it; one because he was too poor, one because he was thin, another because he had scars on his face. Like a good daughter, Abra had always been obedient, for she knew that a beard cannot teach eyelashes, for it has seen the day after them, though it is longer and grayer."

"That is why," continued Yawovi "when Kossikuma, who came home from the city on every vacation, asked for her hand in marriage, and her mother once more objected, Abra rebelled. After yet another argument, Abra went away to the city to live with her man. Abra is now here, and who better to speak of her troubles than she? So with Togbe's permission and if the assembly allows it, I would call Abra to tell us her story."

I said silently to myself that the situation was quite clear, the power of the Word was already evident. To say that the Word has become incarnate is something quite natural; many times I'd heard that when a child became seriously ill, it was because the parents quarreled frequently, and the harsh insults they aimed at each other became incarnated as a disease in the child's body. Until the parents made peace, the child could not get well.

Abra was introduced before the council and began to narrate her story, but it is true that a man's tongue is like rain in the dry season and a woman's is like rain in the rainy season. After telling us the whole story in great detail, a little weariness crept into the assembly; some had begun animated discussions amongst themselves.

Papa Wadefe had to intervene: "Agoo! Let Togbe hear on behalf the assembly, so that it may come to the minds of all present that the ear unfortunately has only one hole and therefore cannot hear a thousand things at a time."

Then turning to Abra: "We have heard you, we are guests in your house, our throats are a little dry, what do you say?"

At this thinly veiled request, everyone laughed, and Abra immediately had some palm wine brought in. After a short prayer to the ancestors, the village chief poured a few drops on the ground, then the half gourd passed from hand to hand to quench everyone's thirst with the freshly fermented milky wine.

Papa Wadefe resumed, "Togbe, hear for Abra and Yawovi, our elders say that the tongue sits in the middle of the teeth, but sometimes the teeth can wound it; on the other hand, to make reconciliation, you don't bring a knife that cuts, but a needle that sews, and if you have to sharpen a knife, you can't sharpen only one side. Therefore, you must hear the other side as well."

With that, a discussion began of relatives and acquaintances, those who thought like Abra, and others who thought like old Nukuku, reproaching the daughter for her ingratitude, for having run off to the city to lead who knew what kind of life, for leaving the old woman alone and never returning to see her, never sending any sign of life.

The discussion went on like this until the sun set; we stopped just long enough to eat a plate of *fufu*,[3] freshly pounded by the women, seasoned with a sauce made of palm nuts. Meanwhile the palm wine, both fresh and distilled, poured out like a river. As the red sun went off wrapped in its sheets of white clouds, and the minds began to blur and the tongues of those who spoke began to mellow, Papa Wadefe asked permission of the village chief to postpone the discussion until the next day.

We returned home, my father and I, exhausted and silent, each of us absorbed in his own thoughts.

The next day at dawn we were all back in Nukuku's courtyard discussing the account. Once again, we heard much the same things, just recounted in different words, colored by different sayings and proverbs.

---

3   A West African dish made from mashed yams, cassava roots, and/or plantains.

Around noon, Papa Wadefe intervened to say that we had heard enough and reminded everyone that "death does not take advice, nor blows the horn" and that "while it takes much time for something to grow, it takes little time for it to die" and therefore a decision had to be made quickly before the irreparable occurred.

During the night, the elderly Nukuku's condition had worsened, as well as that of her daughter Abra, who was now bedridden and feverish.

It is true that "a cola nut in the mouth of a neighbor doesn't seem bitter" and that "the tooth only aches in the mouth of he who has the rotten tooth," but the call of Papa Wadefe brought us back to the tension and gravity of the situation.

After an hour of counsel, we agreed that "the thorn will come out the same way it went in." While there was still time, we had to convince the elderly Nukuku to retract her fateful phrase.

To this day, I still don't understand why the council chose Papa Wadefe and me: I, who was at my first council and had not even uttered a single word. I don't know why they chose us to go and talk to the suffering old woman.

When we entered her room, the contrast of the brightness of the courtyard with the darkness of her room did not allow me to see her at first. As my eyes slowly grew accustomed to the darkness and the faint light of the oil lamp, I saw her lying on her mat, folded in fetal position. One of the women caring for her drew near to her ear and said, "Sister Nukuku, we have visitors, Papa Wadefe and Fofoé's son have come to see you."

Papa Wadefe said, "No, I have only come to accompany the young son of Fofoe who has a few things to say to you."

At these words, I felt my tongue become heavy and wooden, while my legs began to tremble.

Gathering my courage, I approached the elderly Nukuku, took both her hands between mine, and said: "Mama Nukuku, I have come to speak to you as your grandson, Abra's son, would speak to you. It is true that once you have spit out your saliva, you cannot swallow it again, but leaning against your neighbor's barn will never fill your belly. Abra's death would certainly not give you your life back, but it would leave your grandson alone. What will become of him? You know better than I that one pole does not make a house, and that a mother who is not yours does not understand your hunger.

"A bird does not fly with the wings of another, and in order to move forward, life does not turn its head backwards; it is right that when the elephant dies, its tusks remain. Consider well, mama, and forgive because in the direction you are headed, resentment will not keep away the cold of night. Squeeze my hand if you want us to understand that you forgive, squeeze my hand!"

I said nothing more because there was nothing more to say, and in the stillness of the silence that permeated the room, I felt the blistering gazes of Papa Wadefe and the woman whose hands I held. I could hear old Nukuku's feeble breath growing weaker and I knew she was poised at the ford. Defeated and resigned to destiny, I began to withdraw my hands from hers when suddenly I felt her icy and bare fingers grasp my hands with an unexpected strength. Then, as in a confused dream I saw Papa Wadefe jump up, run from the room and shout, "Come quickly, she retracted, she retracted."

He then ran back into the room with a half gourd of water in one hand and a leaf of grass in the other. He shredded the leaf until its juice dripped into the water and, aided by the neighbor woman, lifted Nukuku's frail, pallid head to rinse out her mouth, to wash away forever those dreadful words spoken years ago.

The Word, the Word, the Power of the Word makes it so that even today when someone says to another, "I'll never speak to you again," they don't talk to each other anymore. In order to be able to speak together again, one must cleanse the temple of the word, wash out one's mouth to purify it of the words that had been spoken.

As I walked out of the elderly Nukuku's room, I felt drained, I staggered in the bright, blinding light of the courtyard.

I looked for my father in the crowd that had poured into the courtyard from the neighborhood with celebratory shouts, overwhelming the council. Papa Wadefe, coming out in his turn, took me gently under his arm and brought me before Togbe, whose wrinkled face was bright and laughing. Finally, I found my father looking at me. He approached me without a word, his eyes spoke for him. Then he took me by the hand and led me to my chair. As I sat down, I realized that I had finally earned my place on the village council of wise men.

The elderly Nukuku left us that night to cross the river. And Abra? On the following day, Abra's fever broke.

"When memory hunts for wood to warm itself with nostalgia, it chooses only the best logs." Still, I remember that with us, the Word is a sacred thing.

HOME . . . SICKNESS

Of all the years I've spent in Italy, I wouldn't know which one is to blame for what's happening to me now. I know I should decide once and for all; I should cut the umbilical cord that binds me to this bad habit, this sort of sickness. I can't even remember how it all started, though it must have been after I returned to Togo from Italy.

"Italy!" In those days just thinking of the possibility was like touching the sky. For years my brother Fofo had been promising that he'd bring me to Europe with him. I don't even know how to describe my joy when that long-awaited letter finally arrived. My cousin who lived in the city brought the letter to us, since his mailbox served as the *refugium peccatorum* for all of the correspondence from our relatives and everyone else in the village.

My father was reluctant.

"A girl traveling to the Whites' country all alone! Don't even think about it!"

My mother took my side.

"She's not going alone, she's going to meet her brother!" When her husband repeated: "Don't even think about it!" she nodded at me to leave the room, and that nod comforted me because, appearances aside, I knew who wore the pants in our house.

The very next day my mother took me to the market to buy a suitcase, some second-hand slacks, and my father went to town to get all the documents required for the trip.

The night before leaving I saw tender tears mark my mother's face and I had a fleeting sense of guilt, knowing that I was leaving her alone to do all the work in the fields and the house. Papa withdrew into a defensive silence until the last moment, then, while saying goodbye, he put a talisman of inlaid leather into my hand with a shell and muttered, "Take care of yourself."

Italy! God, the cold! I never imagined it could be so cutting. My lips chapped, my fingers froze, and my skin took on that lizard gray, though I slathered myself with coconut lotion. The first night was infernal, I spent it in a hotel in Rome where my brother had made a reservation for me: I was half-frozen, lying on top of the bed as I used to do on the mat at home, not knowing that I was supposed to crawl under the sheets. Fofo explained it the next day and laughed at me when he picked me up at the station in Bergamo.

My brother sent for me to look after his children and take care of the house because he and his wife both worked. He, his Italian wife, and their two children lived in Torre Boldone, a little town not far from Bergamo where he was a doctor. They'd prepared a room for me in the basement. It was obvious that they were doing well, even though I saw that my brother was a little henpecked. Just like my mother, his wife was the one in charge, only here more overtly so.

It was difficult at first to communicate with my sister-in-law and niece and nephew because I couldn't understand the language and my brother refused to act as translator.

The one thing he immediately did do was give me a set of rules: keep my room clean, wear the "house skates" when I went into the living room, don't take a shower every day because the heating costs were high, don't leave the lights on over the stairs or in the bathroom, don't take three hours to finish the ironing, don't speak our language, and keep the volume low on my "African funeral music." Included in this list of commandments was the prohibition on preparing foods that took too long to cook and especially foods that filled the house for days with the aroma of spices ("that stink").

I spent days agonizing over my mistakes, like crunching on the bones during a meal, something my brother loved to do back home. Why was it that here it seemed to call up some sense of shame for him?

I didn't know my brother anymore: he let his children call him by his first name as if he were some school friend. He and his wife gave into them for everything, they even had to beg those kids to eat meat! They were spoiled rotten. For myself, I would raise my children right (I wanted to have at least six as we do in Africa) and teach them obedience and respect. I didn't like how children talked back to their parents here.

I smile now recalling all of this, at my shock when I first saw my nephew throw one of his temper tantrums because a "little skin" had formed over his milk. When I saw my brother get up, I was happy, thinking of the well-deserved smack he was going to give the boy, but instead, he simply took a spoon to remove the skin and beg the boy, "Come on, sweetie, just drink a little more!"

Horrified! I was completely horrified!

I had to take care of those kids, but I could not get them to mind me. One day when I was beside myself, I screamed at them in my language and they burst out laughing, literally aping my "African talk" with "Abuga bongo bingo!"

"And yet," I thought bitterly, "this is the language of their father's fathers!" But I didn't say another word to them. I didn't know how to act anymore. My sister-in-law made me feel like an intruder, she looked at me suspiciously because, out of politeness, I never looked her in the eyes when I talked to her. One day I heard her tell a friend on the phone that I was sneaky and hypocritical.

My dream of Europe was quickly mutating into a nightmare, too cold, too little time, and then the indifference, the loneliness.

I spent more and more time locked in my room to cocoon myself in memories. I quickly used up the sack of cassava flour and peanuts that my mother had slipped into my suitcase. I couldn't adjust to always eating pasta: even though they said there was a huge difference between tortellini, bucatini, spaghetti, and lasagna, to me it was all pasta. I wanted to taste *la pate*[1] with a hearty sauce of gombo and chicken with a lot of hot pepper, taste it with my hands, take smoking hot handfuls, mince it well, roll it into a ball, and press a deep indentation with my thumb in order to easily gather up all the sauce before swallowing it, then lick my fingers deliciously and crunch on a piece of bone.

I smile today at my shame when my body first saw the moon there and I didn't know what absorbent pads were (I'd brought pieces of cloth with me), or my first adventure buying pantyhose, not knowing that they came in different sizes, colors, and prices.

---

1   A white polenta prepared without salt.

I still see as if it were yesterday, the alarmed face of my sister-in-law when she saw me pull my first attempt at doing laundry out of the washing machine—sweaters that were knotted up and white shirts and underwear had turned pink or were spotted with purple.

I owe my survival to Conception, a Filipino girl who was the housekeeper for the family next door and who spoke a little French. We first saw each other from our balconies while I was trying to beat a carpet, then we met doing the shopping at the supermarket. She'd been in Italy for five years and her friendship and her advice were like manna in the desert.

With her I quickly learned the language, how to cook Italian dishes, and how to keep the house better. I worked quickly so I would have time left to read or watch TV. And very quickly I learned to appreciate the food. I tried to assimilate as much as possible, to completely forget who I was. With time I became more demanding. I wanted my brother to let me go out every so often, I wanted my day off, just like Conception, I wanted money to send a present to my mother or to buy clothes that I liked and not just take my sister-in-law's hand-me-downs. In the arguments born out of this, my brother and I both made accusations I never would have thought possible. He said, "You are ungrateful!" when I told him that I'd found a place working for an elderly woman in Bergamo because I wanted to be independent. At first, he'd shout, "If we'd wanted to pay for a babysitter or housekeeper, we didn't need to bring you all the way from Africa, you know!" Then when he saw the firmness of my decision, he played the emotional card, "So you don't care that you're leaving when we need you, you'd abandon your niece and nephew, you only pretended to care about them! You are completely heartless!"

I alone know what it cost me to leave my brother, resisting the temptation to embrace him, trying to explain to him that I could not come all the way to Europe without at least trying to accomplish something on my own; unlike him, I dreamed of going home someday and creating something of my own. I didn't want to be a servant in a foreign country my entire life.

So one spring day when the morning air stung my face and nostrils, and nature was rising from her dark lethargy with the sprouting of the plants and the sweet birdsong of freedom, I made my flight toward independence. I went to live just outside of Bergamo with Maria, an elderly lady who cleared my residency with the police and got me all of the documents to stay in the country legally. Meanwhile, I enrolled in a sewing course and saved my money in order to buy a sewing machine all my own.

After the first period of anger passed and after a letter from our father, my brother came to visit me unbeknownst to his wife. There at my new home, I found again the Fofo I had always known; we spoke our own language, I cooked our food for him, hot and spicy, which he scooped up with his hands and swallowed greedily . . . with his hands, he snapped bones with his teeth and sucked out the marrow, making an infernal noise, and I even heard him laugh as we do at home, a belly laugh, and talk, and remember people and events from our village. One day watching him let loose and dance to the rhythm of our traditional music, I laughed at him, "Doctor, if your patients could just see you now!"

And he laughed, "They would say, 'And yet you seemed like one of us!'"

He left with a light heart and with the ironic glint in his eye of someone who'd had fun betraying himself.

My friend Conception came to visit me every other Sunday and together we'd fantasize about everything we wanted to accomplish once we'd returned home permanently. My idea was to start a co-op of tailors and make European-style clothes with African fabrics, maybe even to sell to the big distributors in Europe . . .

I also had the opportunity to meet other compatriots and started speaking with the other Africans that I met on the street. Some came to visit me, because I was lucky enough to have my own apartment on the first floor of the house where we could be together and braid hair, listen to music without disturbing anyone, talk out loud. Our meetings were my only chance to show off my flashy *bubu*.

Signora Maria was genuinely kind. One night while she was embroidering the thousandth doily, bent over the lace pillow with tired eyes, she confided in me that we had brought light and the joy of living back into her house even though initially, seeing us talking and gesturing from a distance, it looked like we were arguing.

One day Fofo found me at home with some of my girlfriends dancing to a piece of music from our country. When he arrived, a silence fell out of respect but one also full of reproof because many considered him a traitor. Not so much because he'd married a white woman, but because, they said, he'd become like the Whites: cold and indifferent toward his people, as if he were ashamed of his origins. And also no one understood why, with all the room he had in his big house, he never organized an occasional evening to dance, not even on important holidays. He felt uncomfortable and after a little while he ran off with the excuse of needing to see a patient. From then on, he started to call before stopping by, as they do in Europe. I'm not defending him, but I understood that he'd made the choice to stay permanently in Italy; to keep peace in his family, he'd sunk to making personal compromises.

Knowing my sister-in-law, I understand that he couldn't bring "people" home with no warning as we do at home or invite them to lunch or dinner or even to spend the night. Here everything is different. At home, being used to big families and due to the fact that we eat just one course, usually with a sauce for a base, it's easy to heat up a little more, or to stir some *pate* in a pan or crush up some *fufu*[2] to make room for one more guest around the table. Some people blamed my sister-in-law, but I believe it's the pace of life here that dilutes feelings, devouring life and people. And if it was fine with him like this, as he confided to me one day, it should be fine with us, as he claimed he had the right to live his life as an individual and not as part of a collective as African solidarity required, and besides, he didn't feel obligated to associate with someone simply because that person was black or came from Africa.

"Here in Europe," he pontificated, "everyone must think of himself, end of story. I only feel a duty toward my close relatives, and only if they are in need and are deserving."

Clearly, I didn't share his point of view. I only replied, "Fofo, this country, this fog, it's not for me. I miss the sunshine, the holidays in the village, the weather, the laughter, living together with others."

---

2 A West African dish made from mashed yams, cassava roots, and/or plantains.

And still, I went on working, saving, suffocating my homesickness with a single goal: returning home and opening my tailor shop.

Then two years ago, with a lump in my throat I embraced Signora Maria who had been so good to me, knowing that my departure corresponded with her entering a nursing home. Holding back my growing tears with difficulty, I said good-bye to my brother, to Conception, and to all my friends, and I went "home" with my suitcase full of gifts, plates, silverware, and a dream to fulfill.

After returning to Togo, the first week evaporated away before I understood that I could no longer live in the village where there were no lights and no running water, as I had become used to certain conveniences. I could no longer even start a decent conversation with my girlfriends from before; by now they had gotten married and some already had two or three children and I felt they envied me maliciously. My aging parents insisted that they wanted to choose a man for me to marry, but I had already decided on the liberated life of a single person; I didn't want to be any man's servant and even less did I want to give up my plans.

I decided to move to the city, partly to avoid the daily assault by swarms of relatives who came asking for something, and partly because the heat, the flies, and the mosquitoes had become unbearable to me and I needed to live in an atmosphere that was air conditioned, clean, and calm.

The first year was not very easy, but slowly I managed to build up a steady clientele and one of my clients, Sonia, who had a hair styling salon opposite my shop, had become my confidant. Sonia is a shapely girl, nice and determined; she returned from Germany where she'd worked in the escort business and came back to invest all of her savings in her salon.

Now things are going better for me.

Honestly, I would have to say, things would go even better for me now if it weren't for this strange sense of restlessness that every now and again invades me down to my very bones. In moments like that, I take my car, I go downtown and look around the shops, I go to the grocery store and buy some spaghetti, some cans of tomatoes, some meat imported from France, some taleggio cheese, then I go home to cook it all up and invite Sonia to have dinner with me. Sometimes we go to have a cocktail at the Gattobar, run to devour a pizza from Da Silvia, then finish off the evening with a nice movie starring Mastroianni and Sofia Loren. Sometimes we stay at my house and look at all of my photos from when I was "home" in Italy, listening to the songs from Sanremo, the music of Baglioni, Ramazzotti, or Zucchero.

Sundays, I drive all the way across the city to attend Mass in the parish with the Combonian missionary priests so I can talk with them a little in Italian afterwards.

Sometimes it's Sonia who invites me to have a beer at the Bavaria, the tavern for the German sailors, whom she astonishes with her perfect German, then we go to her house to eat sausage with sauerkraut and mustard and dance Viennese waltzes.

I don't know how to explain this weakness, this mania that I can't seem to get rid of, and which even makes me root for the *Azzurri*[3] when there is an international soccer match. Once after an Italy vs. Germany game, Sonia and I didn't speak to each other for a week.

Ah, Italy! To think that in Italy I wanted so much to go home! Now I feel like a tenant in two countries: sometimes I'm happy for that, other times I feel divided, a little unbalanced, as if a part of me remained there, and yet I know that there I would still have suffered from "*mal d'Africa*."

Maybe it's just nostalgia, or maybe it's "*mal di . . . mal di . . . Europa*."[4]

---

3   National soccer team of Italy.

4   The term "*mal d'Africa*" was used by Italians to express nostalgia for a colonial life, or for the exotic life they had in Africa.

TWO BOXES OF MATCHES

When the dark night comes
Words will stumble
We will no longer be able to deceive sleeplessness
With our dreams.
When the dark night comes
Intertwining desires
My rough hands
Will flood your lap
With petals of regret
My love,
Before the dark night comes
Give me a pastel child
A watercolor child
A rainbow child . . .
To brighten the dark night.

On the way back from the cemetery Francesca's mother said uncertainly, "Stay with us for a while . . ."

Knowing her daughter, she already knew what the answer would be, "No. No, mom. I'm fine, don't worry . . . life goes on."

And stroking her protruding belly, she repeated even more softly, "Life goes on."

On the day after her husband's funeral, Francesca Marelli awoke from a dreamless sleep. Despite the advanced state of her pregnancy, she got up quickly without glancing at the empty space beside her in the bed.

In the bathroom, at the sight of their two toothbrushes, the thought of her husband pierced her heart. Powerful and sharp, the vivid memory of his tender voice on their wedding day, "Francy, I, Togbé, only son of Atsu Kwami and Ami Dzatugbé, swear that my heart will be yours forever."

Francesca ran her icy hand over her face to chase away that voice. She dressed quickly. On the desk she found one of those envelopes reinforced with plastic and bubble wrap. She took one of the two matchboxes that were sitting in the dresser drawer, and before putting it inside the envelope, she pressed it to her heart, and then kissed it. She sealed the envelope, wrote her in-laws' address on it, and left for the post office to mail it to Atsu and Ami.

From her late husband's stories, Francesca understood:

> *Four times Atsu and Ami saw their dream of having children vanish: once at the third month, once at the seventh, once at the eighth and once at the ninth. Some men claimed that Atsu's blood was too strong. Atsu's aunts offered to look for a second wife for him. Some women in the marketplace whispered, furtively pointing to the old woman Kuno who lived alone on the edge of the village. Tongues murmured that to appease her fetishes, the old woman would devour children with her eyes right from their mothers' wombs.*
>
> *After trying every concoction and various sacrifices, Atsu and Ami decided to go and consult the soothsayer to learn the reason for the deaths of their unborn children so they could eliminate the evil that was devastating them and to understand if it was a curse cast by the evil eye of a sorcerer. At the end of the divining ritual, the soothsayer gave some herbs to Ami to chew during her pregnancy, a potion to make for her morning bath with water that had sat under the full moon, and advised her to enact the ceremony of the "hidden child" as soon as the baby was born.*
>
> *So, one Friday morning, Atsu's wife, who hadn't seen the moon for nine months, went up on the roof, and without letting an ant or mouse in the thatched roof hear her pain, came down with a strong baby.*

When Ami went into labor, and the baby was close at hand, the old midwife of the village asked the young man Djifa to go and hide in the bush not far from the houses where the paths to the fields and the river met.

The newborn baby was separated from the placenta: "the real mother" that the aunts went to bury in the right direction, so the couple could have more children in the future. The midwife then wrapped the newborn baby in cloth, set him in a basket, and placed it by the river near Djifa's hiding place. As soon as she heard a passerby coming, the woman turned her back and took two steps as if to leave.

Suddenly, the passerby was heard shouting in surprise, "I've found a baby! I've found a child!"

At that moment Djifa also came out of his hiding place, jumping and shouting with indescribable joy. The people from huts nearby rushed out and then all together, they returned home. The person who found the baby became an assumed relative of the newborn child and consequently was the one to give it a name. The passerby gave the baby back to the midwife saying: On my return from the fields, I found this creature. I come to entrust it to you. Take good care of him so that he may grow in health and wisdom. Since I have found him, we will call him "Fofo," that is "foundling." They also gave him the name Koffi because he was born on a Friday. After this ceremony, he was safe and sound."

"Then why is it that you're called Togbé?" Francesca asked him, keenly.

"Patience, Francy, I'm telling you . . ."

Togbé loved to recount stories, to feel the words in his mouth, to narrate with a wealth of detail, sometimes even to the point of imitating the characters, of impersonating the protagonists' various tones of voice.

He continued:

"It's a boy! A beautiful baby boy!" the midwife's cry of joy rose from the hut along with the cries of the newborn.

"God, he looks so much like my late brother!" Aunt Afi commented.

"Yes, he really is the picture of Kuaku!" affirmed old Osofo with his toothless smile.

Emotion and pride were painted on the usually imperturbable face of the young Atsu.

Everything would have been ideal if not for the fact that the baby refused to nurse and cried constantly. After three days, his skin had wrinkled so much that you could count his ribs with the naked eye. He cried all night long; he never slept, and he never let anyone else sleep.

After a week of this hellish life, his parents and aunties began to cast about to find the cause for the little heir's constant complaints.

"Let's go consult the soothsayer, and let's go soon," said Aunt Afi, "because a tree can hide a forest."

"Surely he will be able to recognize the 'dzoto'[1] of our son," announced Uncle Atsutsé in a grave voice.

In the process of the divining ritual, the spirit of grandfather Kuaku took possession of the body of the soothsayer while in a trance and announced, "Koffi is the son of my son and yet he is the father of his father, for he is my reincarnation. Go to my hut. On a wall you will find my bracelet hanging, put it around the baby's neck and cover him with my holiday kente for six months and then I will be able to return to live among you."

Koffi's crying ceased that same evening; he began to take his mother's milk and soon gained weight.

Atsu organized a banquet to celebrate. The whole extended family was invited to attend, to eat and drink in order to welcome the child whom from that day on everyone began to call "Togbé," which means "grandfather."

---

1   The guardian ancestor.

"And that's why your name is Togbé!" Francesca concluded eagerly. Ignoring her interruption her husband continued unperturbed:

> *At dawn on the eighth day after my birth, I was brought to Uncle Atsutsé by old Agbanavon for the rite of circumcision. According to tradition, an uncircumcised boy will never become a man. On the eve of the ceremony, Uncle Atsutsé did not need to warn Agbanavon, as tradition recommended, not to lie with a woman during the night, for to do so would bring misfortune on the ceremony. Though the wise Agbanavon liked to joke that not even the fondest of memories would warm his blood.*
>
> *When we arrived at the old man's dwelling, I was brought to the hut with the tron at the entrance, the voodoo of the ancestors. I was sprinkled with succulent plants soaked in water from dew collected in the terracotta basin placed on top of three crossed trunks at the entrance to the ceremonial room . . .*

"And on that day," Togbé concluded, "I became a man who was prepared to meet his *sé*."[2]

No one could have known then that destiny would lead him to cross the ocean by means of an iron bird, that vast water that boils without any fire under it. No one could have imagined that there in the countries of white-skinned men, he would meet the love of his life and also meet his death. Not even Francesca Marelli was expecting that man, the man she had loved at first sight and the man whom a cruel fate snatched away from her after only two years of life together.

Inevitably, her memory brought back that first train trip from Milan to Asso.

---

2   From Ewe, a term for destiny.

She saw him again with his proud face absorbed in reading a French magazine. The only empty seat was right next to him. When she approached, he glanced up briefly and their eyes met. She was surprised to hear herself asking in French, "*C'est libre?*"[3]

It was like an enchantment to watch his face, which had seemed so serious, brighten with a smile so child-like and disarming that it melted her heart.

"*Oui*! How is it you speak French?"

She explained to him that she was majoring in Languages at Università degli Studi di Milano Statale. He expressed surprise: it was rare to meet Italians who spoke the language of Molière so well. When he'd arrived in Italy three years earlier, he'd assumed it would be otherwise, given the proximity to France.

She blushed with pleasure.

As they came up on the station at Meda, she told him her name was Francesca, and he commented, "Francesca, Françoise . . . yes, it's clear that France, the French language must be your destiny."

They talked as if they'd known each other for a long time. She, whom everyone described as introverted and reserved, surprised herself by confiding her dreams. By the time they reached the Canzo station, Francesca learned that he was from Togo, that he'd left his homeland to teach French in nearby Ghana, then left for Senegal and the Ivory Coast where he'd taught English. Next he went to Libya, where he'd met some Italians with whom he'd go on to Italy. He was now working at a company in Canzo where they made scissors.

Even though she was headed to Asso, when Togbé got off at Canzo, she got off with him, and they walked together to the next station.

Francesca remembered how her mother probed over dinner that evening, with that instinct only a mother possesses: "What's wrong with you today? You seem out of sorts."

"Me, nothing! Nothing, mom, it's just life as usual."

So many train rides! So many rendezvous comprised of words, of silences and listening, curious glances, mischievous smiles filled with subtext as well as understanding and fondness.

---

3   "Is this seat free?"

On that night of dense fog, after Togbé, feverish, closed his eyelids to this life, Francesca curled up near the lit fireplace and desperately sought some heat to warm her pain-chilled soul. She stared as the blue flickers were born and watched them flare into yellow-orange flames feverishly licking at the dry wood that crackled joyfully into a thousand sparks, making the logs burn bright red. Slowly they turned black with smoke. When a flame seemed about to die, a twig was enough to tease it back to life.

Filling herself with courage, she picked up the phone and called Togbé's parents. In the silence of the night, the still incredibly youthful voice of Togbé's mother reached Francesca's ear from Africa, clear, quiet, sweet.

When she announced the terrible news, Ami could only emit a strangled, "Oh!"

After a long silence, the elderly Ami asked in a hoarse voice, "My child, where are you now?"

"I am here alone in our house in front of the fireplace. I just wanted to be alone."

"I understand . . ."

After a long pause filled with sighs and suppressed tears, Ami continued, "You see my daughter, our lives are similar to those of the logs in the hearth: a breath is enough to light them up, some burn and bring light and give heat for a long time, others make a lot of smoke and that's all, but a breath is enough to extinguish them or to bring them back to life . . . it's like that in our lives as well; everything depends on our *sé*."

The elderly Ami paused for a moment, took a deep breath and went on, "My child, it is sad for a mother to outlive her child. You know, a child is a dream full of many dreams, a suffering of many pains, nights of wakefulness and anguish over the slightest fever. But a child is joy, it is a privilege for us as women, a gift from the *sé*. The *sé* gives and the *sé* takes away. That is how life is. Many suffer from being far from their loved ones, but for a mother, her child is never far away because he is always alive in her heart. Loved ones die only when we forget them. The *sé* of Togbé wanted him back. It was like uprooting him from my heart, but I know that a living soul is growing in your womb, I know that my son is not dead. On the contrary, his seed has overcome time and the distance of the ocean and will bring forth fruits under other skies in turn that will bring forth many other fruits in many other parts of the earth. I am proud of this today. I am proud because part of me will see things that I do not know, and that I dare not even dream of. Don't be afraid; his blood, our blood, is strong blood." She concluded, asking, "Did my son tell you what to do?"

"Yes, he told me about the matchboxes."

"That's good. Now hugs to you. Be strong! We're waiting. And I'm handing the phone to papa, he wants to talk to you."

When the call was over, Francesca, mindful of their instructions, took a pair of scissors and approached the lifeless body of her companion.

Carefully, she cut his nails and hair, made two tiny piles, wrapped them in two small squares of white cloth and placed them in two matchboxes. She packaged it and made it ready to send to the family back home.

Togbé used to tell her, "If I should die here in your country, please do not spend money sending my body home: wherever one dies, the flesh dissolves permanently into the earth. You only need to send my fingernails and hair because we believe that they contain one's vital energy, because only they continue to grow throughout life. The immaterial, immortal soul will return after forty days to *Tséfé*[4] in the company of our relatives and friends. I only ask you to inform them, so that they can hold a funeral. Otherwise, my soul will remain lost and silent, wandering disconsolate and will be unable to participate in any happiness in the afterlife. If you observe the ritual, my breath of life can continue to roam the earth before being reincarnated one day in the body of an infant in my family."

Francesca hated such talk and tried to avoid it, tried to check him with the plea, "Please, stop it. You know how this kind of talk scares me."

But he continued in a calm, deep voice, "You see my love, although we are born to die, though life belongs to death, death is never an end in itself. We are all just souls forever journeying."

That day Francesca went out to mail one matchbox.

---

4   The land of the dead.

*

When she reached full term, Francesca gave birth to a beautiful baby boy weighing eight pounds, nine ounces. At the birth, Francesca's mother looked at her grandchild, and exclaimed with her arched eyebrows, "But . . . he's white!"

After a moment of surprised silence, Francesca broke into laughter and explained with tears in her eyes, "Please, mom, don't worry, I promise he's Togbé's son: his skin will darken in two or three days."

She gave him the name Apélété as her father-in-law Atsu had suggested during their brief phone conversation, "You see Francesca, our son is gone, leaving your house empty, unsafe and desolate. When the fruit you now carry in your womb is born, if it is a boy you should name him Apélété for that means 'the house is standing.' If it is a girl, you should name her Ahuefa which means 'peace is in the house.' This is how our customs are; you will see that you will be revived."

But in the first days after the baby's birth, anguish tunneled into Francesca's soul. Baby Apélété was driving the staff in the nursery crazy and kept the whole wing of the hospital awake with his constant cries. He wouldn't latch on to nurse and refused the formula that they tried to give him with the bottle.

The doctors grew seriously concerned about his weight loss; it had gone beyond the physiological limit and was endangering his life. The staff was beginning to consider giving him an IV.

On the third night, Francesca dreamt of her deceased partner and everything became as clear to her as water flowing smoothly over a rock.

When she awoke, Francesca called home and asked her mother to bring one of her late husband's shirts. When her mother arrived, Francesca went to the bassinet where little Apélété was screaming convulsively, red in the face. There, under the astonished looks of the staff, she gently placed the shirt on the child and it was like a miracle: hiccupping, he calmed down and stopped screaming. Francesca took him in her arms and finally he latched onto his mother's breast, sucking voraciously on his mother's milk.

Shortly after, he fell blissfully asleep in his bassinet under her loving gaze, fists closed, arms folded over his head.

Francesca's mother gazed at the newborn in disbelief, "God! He looks just like his father!"

"Yes," Francesca nodded with a smile, "He really is my Togbé."

When she returned from the hospital, Francesca's mother saw her daughter burying a box of matches in the garden under the tree where, in the summer, her husband used to relax for a nap.

When she asked, "What's that, Francesca?"

"Nothing! Nothing, mom, it's just life that goes on."

"My child . . . I think you have become like them."

"You think so? Yes, maybe a little."

NIGHT

Elom Doglo was awakened by the violent slamming of the shutters left half-open to catch what little breeze there was. He woke up drenched in sweat and pushed back the sheets. He heard the wind, as if afflicted by some dark evil, howling and moaning through the grates. Immediately Elom was overwhelmed by a ceaseless anguish. His thoughts had already begun feverishly chasing each other in waves. Cascading in an avalanche, they crashed down on his obsessive mind: farewell to slumber.

Suddenly, the air lashed into in the room like a fury, violently unfurling itself. A trapped fugitive, it searched for a way out, desperately lifting the roof tiles. Startled, the gears of Elom's brain started turning again, where the memories, the ideas rose like bubbles, magnetically attracted to one another, merging into bigger bubbles that burst then crystallized. Sometimes it seemed that his mind barely brushed against a light, a truth. Then everything vanished and the frustration, boredom, the pain of being, of living, returned. It felt like he was traveling in a familiar direction but then, always and inescapably, he got off at the wrong station. Or worse: it seemed like he constantly missed his train or his connection. And so his thoughts quietly evaporated, leaving an emptiness inside him where his anxieties curled up to stay.

In the distance, the sky muttered. The rain came down to water the ground. The air expanded with the acrid scent of hot, smoking asphalt.

Elom Doglo sat on the edge of the bed, his head hanging down. A muffled clap of thunder echoed in the distance. He rose to go out on the balcony. He was immediately struck by a louder clap of thunder and dazzled by a blue flash that tore across and wounded the darkness of the night. Slowly the rumbling receded with echoes like a flock of planes. Elom saw the stereo display flash: the power had gone out. Blinded by the lightning, he felt the darkness of the night.

And then the rain, which before had fallen in thick, heavy tears, became as fine and frustrating as the spray from an encrusted showerhead. The heavy air became warm, then gradually cooler.

Elom felt goose bumps.

He walked back into his room.

The clock on the dresser read three o'clock in the morning. He went back to bed, pulling the sheets up to cover himself. He curled up, luxuriating in the crisp, warm feeling of being sheltered.

Outside in the howling wind, nature was running wild, marking everything in its path.

He tried to fall asleep again, focusing his mind on a pleasant thought, a happy thought. Unfortunately, the thunderstorm had drawn the curtains of sleep shut, closing off every hope. Shadows of undefined presences now filled the room. Unhealthy fears crowded his mind.

He thought he heard a voice, "Never look at the dark of night when it smiles . . ."

He closed his eyes, tried to escape from himself, from his torment.

Silently his soul slipped into the night. Barefoot in the silence, on the sly, his soul moved around his heart. He discovered an island, alone, deserted.

Elom felt like a comma, an ink stain, black, on a faded page of life.

Stretching his hand towards the other side of the bed, he felt the comforting warmth of Giorgia's body. Giorgia Venanzi had been his partner for four years. Elom felt the steady rise and fall of her back: she remained unaware of the night storm. He caressed the curves of her hips. His fingers lingered to wipe away the beads of sweat that curled into the low valley of her back. She didn't move. He would have loved the comfort of her caresses, the warmth of her body to ease the aching in his soul.

Angst seemed to have settled in every recess of his being, along every fiber of that shell he carried. At the edge of the abyss, with the complicity of the night, he touched her arm. He sought her hand.

He caressed her fingers and she turned over with her back to him, anchoring herself to the mattress. He tried again to reach her hand. She withdrew it and Elom sank into the abyss. He hated the night with its weight pressing down on his chest. He got up and escaped the suffocating grip of those sticky sheets.

Outside, the night tainted the city with a veil of black. Thick, noisy darkness. He didn't know how to compare the burden of solitude with nostalgia for his homeland. Indefinable melancholy was this flame constantly burning under the ashes of daily life in a foreign land, an unrelenting feeling of being nobody, or worse, of not even existing. Elom saw the curious, irritated, or pitying looks from others, felt them slide past him as if he were a shadow.

Exhausting memories intertwined with sounds, noises, smells, scents, colors, laughter. Unexpectedly, then the voice of his grandmother, Mama Amewonò.

She was the one person for whom he'd never needed to show off, the only one who always stood up for him. He used to sit next to her when he felt the stormy air hovering in the house. They didn't need words to understand each other. He would sit brooding in a silence steeped in complicity. Crouching next to her, he drew figures in the sand with a piece of wood while she tirelessly and skillfully twisted the cotton around the spindle to make the thread come to life. From time to time, the old woman would stop and without needing any hint or gesture, he would hand her the small gourd of ground tobacco. She would take a pinch, curve her index finger around the nail of her thumb, and compressing first one nostril and then the other, she would inhale deeply with an "Ah!" of satisfaction. After squeezing her nose, the brownish liquid she sneezed out would drip. She wiped it away with the back of her hand, then wiped her hand on the fabric of her *pagne*,[1] and gratified him with a toothless and knowing smile before going back to spinning.

---

1 An untailored cotton textile.

For a moment it seemed he could hear Mama Amewonò's voice, "Don't look into the dark of night when it smiles . . ."

How he missed his grandmother! Suffocating! The need for tenderness in this foreign land was suffocating. To love and be loved: just five words, a whole life, or rather a whole dream of a life

Existence is a harsh reality. Every one drags himself painfully into the shadows of life, trying on masks adapted to the ephemeral burden of living on improvised stages. To avoid drowning in nostalgia Elom thought, "I should go back to writing. Yes, I'll go back to writing tomorrow and finish that damn novel!"

Writing liberates and defeats loneliness. Writing is a talisman against nostalgia, *ghurba*,[2] *saudade*.[3] It is a way to shout: "I exist, I am here in this society that wants to ignore me in my essence, I am not aphasic, I'm not your object, I'm not a second-class citizen!" Reassured by his decision, he smiled in defiance at the darkness of the room. The shadows thinned. Elom plunged into sleep.

His forehead dripped with sweat in the heat of the packed room.

The powerful beam of a spotlight made the stage as bright as daytime.

He was on the stage. The crowd was cheering. Standing. He couldn't suppress a wide smile. His cheeks were sore with contentment. His novel was a hit. In the back of the room, Giorgia stood apart smiling, proud, her eyes bright. The air smelled of incense. Elom felt light. The president of the jury rang a bell to request silence.

The audience could not stop applauding. The sound of the bell persisted, as irritating as that of an alarm clock. The alarm clock!

---

2 From Arabic, literally estrangement or separation, also used to refer to the state of being or feel like a foreigner.

3 From Portuguese, a sad state of intense longing for someone or something that is absent.

Elom reached out his hand to turn it off. Giorgia was already up. Next to him the empty and crumpled sheets bore the imprints of her body. His brain rumbled inside his head.

"How deluded!" he muttered. A bitter crease froze at the corner of his mouth.

"Never look into the dark of night when it smiles . . . it hides false truths." So said his grandmother's voice.

DEMONSTRATION

"There were lots of us, ten thousand, maybe thirty thousand, maybe one hundred thousand," Yao related, monotone, his eyes fixed on the void, as if he were reliving the nightmare of that afternoon. "So many young people, girls and boys, men and women, all dressed in white, some wearing white shirts, white blouses or white dresses, some wearing white *pagne*[1] like the *wodussi*,[2] some wearing white *boubou*.[3] The order was to wear white."

There were children, running around happily and getting tangled in people's legs, women with sleeping babies strapped to their backs. I'd just gotten to the park and thought things had already started. I was supposed to go with Koffi, and I waited for him at our usual bar, but he didn't come. I had time to swallow two cold beers, but my cousin never showed up.

I looked around for a familiar face. I caught the eye of a young girl four steps ahead of me who had just turned around. She couldn't have been any older than sixteen, seventeen at the most. Her laughing black eyes sparkled, tinged with a wonderful sweetness. She was tall, with slightly prominent cheekbones and hair pulled back to the base of her neck, ebony skin that glistened in the sun's rays. She wore a khaki skirt like schoolgirls, with a white blouse of eyelet, tight across her chest so her nipples protruded provocatively, invitingly. I couldn't help but notice that she wasn't wearing a bra. Before she

---

1   An untailored cotton textile.
2   Novices of voodoo.
3   A flowing wide-sleeved robe.

turned to watch the podium, I aimed a steady look her way and formed an inviting smile.

The atmosphere of the event was jubilant. We felt united in protest, laughing. It was supposed to be a peaceful demonstration. We wanted to take advantage of the visit of a French delegation, to make it clear that we longed for change. We were confident, calm, but determined. The organizers had chosen the square, the garden, instead of the stadium so we couldn't be trapped in an enclosed space when the military came. I kept looking at the back of the girl's head, four rows in front of me, mentally calling to her. I whispered to her, "Turn around, beautiful!" thinking that with the force of my thoughts, I could make her look back.

Thousands of hands were waving white handkerchiefs.

It was just before the start of the rainy season. Huddled together in the stifling afternoon heat, our foreheads, lips, armpits all dripped with sweat. You could hear the rolling sound of tam tams: the party was about to begin. Suddenly, I don't know how, I don't know when, I don't remember if we heard the gunshots or the shouting first, or maybe it was all at once, or maybe it was the wave of people pressing all around that pushed me forward, until suddenly I was standing next to the beautiful stranger. In an instant all hell broke loose, mass confusion. I heard shouting, "Run, run, they're shooting at us!"

I turned around, alarmed. I watched in disbelief, like a slow-motion movie, the sweet-eyed girl slumped to the ground with a groan, and I noticed a red spot growing and widening along her side. I was paralyzed. A man threw himself to the ground. Everyone was shouting, screaming, running, some to the right, some to the left, stepping on each other. A bald man was shouting, looking for his daughter or his wife: "Afi, Afiii!" elbowing his way through the crowd.

Suddenly I realized the enemy was right in our midst. They had infiltrated us, dressed in white like us and could have been anyone, with the difference that they were armed and were cutting us down like grain at the harvest.

I started to run. I saw a child crying, terrified, his arms stretched out next to the lifeless body of a woman. Panicked, I passed him without stopping. To this day, I still carry with me his bewildered, incredulous look, those huge eyes, wide with fear, his tears running down his round cheeks, his nose beginning to dribble and his voice calling "Dada . . . Dada . . . Dada nyé!"[4]

It was only a split second. Yet, that image has remained so sharp in my mind and has come back to haunt me for many nights, robbing me of sleep time and again.

I ran at breakneck speed, stomping, elbowing. I crashed against an outstretched body and fell to the ground. I felt the hardness of the ground painful against my knees and the dust burning my torn hands. I jumped up and strangely, as I started running again, staggering in the dust, all I could think at that tragic moment was that I'd ruined my nice new shirt.

It's strange how the human mind works. Latching onto or remembering some trivial event is like opening a safety valve suddenly: a trickle of thought helps ward off the oppressive anguish of trauma, of the unbearable. At that dreadful moment, I was shaken by a spasm of hysterical laughter, an attempt to restore some kind of balance, or maybe to try to maintain it. I ran into the street in front of the central post office, and continued towards the main market. All around me there was a river of frightened people running, screaming: "...the tanks, the tanks are coming!" All around me, like the frenzy in an anthill, mopeds and cars were whizzing past with all their horns blaring. I crossed the street in front of the nightclub "Le rêve" to get to the Shell gas station and almost got run over by a stupid Vespa. I kept running, even though my legs ached, and a painful stitch was growing in my left side. I only slowed down at the small market near the cemetery by the beach when my heart seemed ready to burst.

My whole body was dripping with sweat. My shirt was soaked and sticking to my skin. Only then did I feel something sticky at the base of the right side of my neck. I brought my hand up mechanically and my fingers brought back a thick substance, a mixture of brain matter and clotted blood. "Oh God! My God!" I screamed, horrified. I started running again as if I'd been bitten by a tarantula; I ran without stopping all the way home, unaware of the

---

4   From Mina dialect, "Mmmaa . . . Mmmaaa . . . My mama!"

curious and astonished looks of passers-by who still didn't know what had happened. My whole body gave off a strong, strange smell: my pants were wet, soaking wet and not just with urine. Pushing hard on the courtyard door, I rushed past my mother's astonished eyes, straight into the bathroom. Almost ripping off my clothes, I threw myself into the shower and scrubbed myself until my skin peeled, to wash away the horror.

Under the icy water I tried to marshal my thoughts.

The first was, "I'm alive, I'm alive!" I touched myself as if to make sure. Then, I began to cry, at first softly, then at the top of my lungs like an orphan child. Tears, cries of pain, anger, powerlessness, brought my mother. She'd been late, as always, and this time, fortunately for her, had still been preparing to join us at the demonstration.

"Son, what is it?"

"The military," I managed as I shut off the faucet, catching my breath, not even thinking about covering my nakedness.

"The military? At the demonstration?"

"They wanted to kill us, they were killing us, they shot so many people. Mama, it's horrible, they want to kill us . . . they want to kill us!"

At this point in his story, Yao stopped. He began to rock back and forth with his gaze fixed on emptiness, wiping the right side of his neck with his strong, square hand in automatic, repetitive gestures.

The head of the commission of inquiry, who was conducting the investigation into the "alleged massacre" in the gardens, yawned, scratched his beard then ran his finger through the collar of his shirt, looking glumly at the ceiling and the lazy movement of the fan's blades and asked in a slow, detached tone:

"Young man, did you see the shooter?"

"No, sir, but I saw that girl die and all those dead bodies on the ground, all that blood, innocent blood on the white clothes, bodies and blood, that little boy crying . . ."

"Did you see the tanks arrive, the military?"

"No, I didn't see them, I was running, we were all running. There was such a mad confusion . . . but I heard the shouting, 'The tanks are coming!'"

"But you, did you see them?"

"No sir."

"All right," the commissioner concluded loudly. "You can go now."

Then turning to the other members, he announced: "Unreliable witness."

On his way out, Yao heard the soldier standing guard in front of the door shout: "Next!"

YÉVI-THE-SPIDER

"People, hear my tale!
   "We welcome your tale."

My tale starts with the thread of time as it runs . . . runs . . . as it winds through mountains, rivers, valleys, and lands on Yévi-the-spider, Yévi-big-bellied, the black spider.

It was the time of the great famine. In the dry season, the sun dried up the rivers, the streams, the land cracked, there was not one blade of grass. The granaries in the village were empty. Hearts dried up. The men and the animals (who at that time lived in harmony) decided by mutual agreement to choose one to send in search of food. Yévi-the-spider, Yévi-big-bellied, known for his courage and cunning, volunteered.

Before leaving at dawn, Yévi the black spider went to greet the spirits of the ancestors who entrusted him with a cowrie[1] and a kola nut, and warned him, "Son, take these and when you are in need, throw one of them on the ground. Use them one at a time. Now go and know that wherever you go, we, the fathers of your fathers will be with you to protect you."

Yévi walked without stopping. He saw the sun rise then return to bed among the clouds over and over again. He crossed desert plains populated only by animal carcasses, passed by bare trees whose naked arms stretched out pleadingly towards the sky, caressed by the dusty and mournful howl of the wind.

---

1   A shell which served as a form of money in various societies for centuries and are now used in divination ceremonies.

One evening, exhausted, Yévi-the-spider, Yévi- . . . no-longer-so-big-bellied, came upon a prosperous land. There, as far as the eye could see, stretched fields filled with wheat, millet, and sorghum.

For a long time, the inhabitants of this land of plenty had been unable to sleep. Over time, they had become gloomy and sad. They no longer said hello to one other; they no longer laughed. They thought only of working and earning more money. They worked all night and rested during the day, trying in vain to fall asleep.

When he entered the village, Yévi-the-spider, Yévi-the-empty-bellied spotted the elders sitting and chatting under the baobab tree. He approached them with his eyes respectfully downcast and greeted them, "It is evening!"

A reproachful silence, heavy with indignation, came in answer: they were offended that he had spoken to them. And without any explanation, they hauled him before the king to be judged.

Yévi tried to defend himself, "I beg the assembly to hear my humble voice, so that it may reach the heart of your wise sovereign to explain to him that, where I come from, it is our custom to greet each other as a sign of friendship and respect."

They answered him brusquely, "Stranger, if you find yourself among squatting toads, you must not ask for a chair! You deserve death."

Magnanimously, instead they condemned him to two weeks of hard labor by day in the royal fields located behind the king's palace.

Working during the day, he didn't see a soul, except for the graceful silhouette of a young girl who appeared from time to time at a window of the palace. Yévi fell in love with her.

After a week, homesickness and loneliness ate away his heart. Distraught, he threw the cowrie to the ground and a beautiful bird with a multicolored coat appeared before him.

"I am so lonely, my friend, sing for me, sing to keep me company."

In a soft voice the bird sang a beautiful song to the rhythm of sadness:

I come from far away, I left mother and brothers to find food . . .
In my homeland, each snake crawls in its own way.
I come from afar, and in my homeland, it is not because he walks
*   backwards that the shrimp has lost his way . . .*

In the nearby palace of the monarch, the princess, who suffered like everyone else from insomnia, heard the sweet, lonely melody and lulled by the music she fell asleep.

When night fell and she awoke as radiant as the coral tree, she ran to tell her father what had happened. Astonished and hopeful, the sovereign promised vast riches and the hand of his daughter to the one who possessed such power.

It is well-known that flies pounce where there is food, so the next day the palace was invaded by suitors of all kinds, but not one was able to perform the miracle.

After he served his time, Yévi learned of the king's promise.

He immediately went to the court.

The guards stopped him, "Beggars, delinquents, and foreigners are not allowed!"

Yévi-the-spider, Yévi-the-cunning did not lose heart. Turning the corner, he threw the kola nut to the ground and was immediately transformed into a handsome young man.

When he was presented at court, he recognized the princess and asked to be allowed to speak to her privately. Once they were alone, he had her close her eyes and threw the cowrie on the ground.

The rainbow-robed bird sang:

> *I come from far away, I left mother and brothers to find food . . .*
> *In my homeland, each snake crawls in its own way.*
> *I come from afar, and in my homeland, it is not because he walks*
> *   backwards that the shrimp has lost his way . . .*

The pleasant, melancholy song moved the princess. But when she opened her eyes and saw the bird and the black spider, she shrieked. At once, the guards ran into the room followed by the king. There, they surrounded Yévi, ready to club him.

"Stop!" ordered the princess, "He's the one I've been looking for. I'm going to marry him."

"But he's not one of us!" protested the guards.

"I will marry him. His heart is generous."

"He's a spider, and a small one at that, and besides . . . he's black!" they objected.

"Though it's small, a peppercorn is strong, thanks to its spicy flavor."

"But he doesn't know our customs; that was obvious as soon as he arrived . . . "

"Well, we don't know his either!" interjected the king emphatically. "We'll learn from him and he'll learn from us, because when the jaw and the jawbone meet, they break a bone. One hand alone cannot wash itself: to clean itself well, it must rub against another."

The word of a king is sacred. Wisdom sheds light in the darkness.

The two married and there was a great feast indeed.

Yévi-the-spider, Yévi-now-big-belly sent food home.

In the kingdom they went back to sleeping and laughing.

Yévi-the-spider, Yévi-happy-heart and the princess had many, many descendants. Just look in the corners of your houses.

"People, have you heard my tale?"

"Yes, we have heard it."

"Then, people, my story ends."

TENDER SHOOTS

The Olum, the rebels of the Lord's Resistance Army, attacked Adak village in Kitgum district at dawn. They caught everyone still asleep. Thirteen-year-old Ogaba had gone outside to relieve himself behind the mud and banana leaf hut when he heard the first screams mixed with the soldiers' orders. The boy tried to hide in the bushes.

The soldiers raided the corn, wheat, and beets from the houses and rounded up the cattle. They killed men and women, set fire to the houses, and gathered the boys and girls in the village square, tying them to one another with a long rope like animals. There was a rustle behind Ogaba; he gasped. The cold muzzle of a soldier's rifle forced him from the bush: "Hey you, come out! Get out here now!"

The soldier shoved a large sack and a heavy cartridge case at him and ordered: "Take it! Let's go!"

Bent under the burden, Ogaba stood in single file with the other boys who were now untied. They started walking, framed by the muzzles of the guns.

There the boy caught sight of his friends a little further ahead, Opiyo and Oryang from the next village standing by Susan, a young girl from his own village. He tried to reach them, but a soldier noticed and kicked him in the shins. The boy fell to the ground.

"Get up or I'll shoot!"

Ogaba hurried back to his place.

The rebels were heading for South Sudan, east of Juba where they'd set up fallback camps in their war against the Ugandan army and where, allied with the Islamic government, they were also fighting the Sudan People's Liberation Army.

*

They marched for the entire day. The air was hot and dry. They crossed swamps, where mosquitoes tormented their skin, before reaching the top of a small rocky hill, and then climbing down the slope. At the bottom of the valley, the row of marching children left the dirt path and walked into the elephant grass, almost two meters high, which nearly choked them. They walked all night. The next morning, they rested for a while before continuing their march through the night once more.

Some tried to escape. They were caught and killed with machetes in front of the others.

Days and days went by without eating anything but leaves and roots during brief stops. They reached Sudan after a week of marching; some children died on the way. Ogaba's legs were swollen, his skin was tight and shiny, and his feet were bleeding.

When they arrived at the camp, they pushed the girls together then called the officers to choose one, even the youngest girls. Susan, thirteen, was carried off by a fat soldier. Shortly after, her harrowing screams gutted the air, then were smothered. Susan came out of the hut sobbing silently with her eyes on the ground, then she lay in the dirt and curled up with her hands cupped between her legs.

The day after the rape, Susan tried to run away when she was sent to gather firewood. She hid in a tree. They searched for her. Ogaba hoped they would not find her. She was caught.

They brought her in front of Ogaba, Oryang, and Opiyo. They tied her hands and forced the boys to kill her.

Commander Dwaka ordered: "Kick her to death!"

"Kill her!" shouted another soldier.

"She's a Longa! She is not an Acholi like you! She's an enemy."

Oryang kicked first, angrily, violently.

Opiyo began to beat her.

Ogaba knew that girl. They were from the same village.

They had always played together regardless of their ethnic difference. Ogaba refused to hit her.

The commander slapped him to the ground and pointed his weapon in his face:

"Either you hit her now or I'll cut off your arm and then I'll blast a hole in your skull!"

Ogaba was forced to do it, with tears of rage and helplessness blurring his vision. His lips were bleeding.

The girl pleaded with the boys a few times, trying to meet their eyes. Between her screams of pain, she asked, "Ogaba, oh, Ogaba, why are you doing this to me? Why?"

"I . . . I have no choice."

They had to or they would be shot.

Little Susan's cries now became muffled into agonized gasps.

None of the boys had the courage to look at her.

Opiyo prayed silently in his heart: "Lord forgive us . . . You know that we did not mean to kill her."

Ogaba thought bitterly for a moment, "Life means nothing."

After killing her, the rebels made him wipe his arms with her blood.

"Then you won't be afraid anymore to die and you won't try to escape," said the commander.

After returning to the base, they began training. Every morning they did military drills, taking apart their weapon then quickly reassembling it. After a week, they were sent to the front. Ogaba was afraid and did exactly what the rebels ordered. He soon learned how to use his rifle and to attack the enemy. Some boys were too weak to carry their weapons and dragged them on the ground. At first, the three boys did not dare to shoot. They were frightened by the noise of the rifles.

When a burst of gunfire mowed down a soldier near Ogaba, he felt the hot, slimy blood splash on his face and uniform, terrified, he started shooting wildly at everything that moved in front of him.

After the first battle, Commander Dwaka declared: "Now you are here, you must forget your village and your family. From now on we are your family. Anyone who talks about his old family or tries to escape will be killed.

"Our great leader Kony is inspired by the Holy Spirit so he has the power to read your thoughts, he can see inside each one of you and he already knows who is thinking of running away."

Terrified, Ogaba forced himself not to think, rumors spreading that some boys had already been killed when Kony declared they had intended to escape.

"Forget your names! You, from now on, you will be called Crazy Rambo," he said, pointing his finger to Ogaba. Then pointing to Opiyo and Oryang respectively, "you are Hitler Killer and you are Man Eater. Understand?" He punctuated the question by firing a burst into the air.

"Yes!"

"Yes!"

"Yes, commander!"

They had been living at the camp for two years now and could no longer remember their real names. Life in the camp was brutal; it hardened their hearts and reduced their minds to a tangle of instinctive impulses. Gradually, the memory of what they had been faded, withered away, melting into that harsh animalistic existence punctuated and marked by a continuous struggle for survival. Their tattered innocence no longer had a past or future; what remained of them seemed wrapped in a wounded casing, like skin scraped raw and irritated by hot pepper.

Many children were sent to the front lines, others worked as spies, messengers, sentries, food and ammunition carriers, servants, and sex slaves. They were made to set mines or clear minefields, forced to sweep the streets with branches or brooms to uncover or set off mines. Their minds were numbed with drugs and alcohol.

Before each battle each one received his portion and whoever dared to refuse was kicked and clubbed. The drugs gave them all a sense of euphoria, a feeling of strength and often hallucinations: the enemies seemed like animals to be killed. Murdering them was not like killing human beings. Everyone obeyed blindly and killed without fear and without realizing what they were doing.

At the camp, the girl prisoners cooked and were worked to exhaustion with a thousand different chores. They were frequently raped and beaten, the forced concubines of the commanders. Some were drafted into military service and learned to kill. Over time they became insensitive to the suffering of others, and even exulted in the prestige and strength conferred by possessing a weapon. They learned how to use any kind of weapon, pistols to Kalashnikovs to machine guns.

The weapon became the only companion to be trusted, the only one who could save your life, day after day. They laid down every night with their weapon clutched to their sides.

At the base, there was never enough food for everyone. Since Crazy Rambo and his friends had done well in the first few fights, they were put into a group that was to go to Uganda to steal food and medicine. They looted all the villages along the way.

The terrified screams from the villagers as they arrived excited them: "The cutters are coming! The *otontongs!*"

This was their nickname because they mutilated with machetes anyone who collaborated with the regular army. Their group was more feared than actual soldiers.

Hitler Killer and Man Eater, in a perpetual state of drug-induced highs, were unable to withstand the tension. They amused themselves by pointing their machine guns at the checkpoints to humiliate civilians of every age, gender, and creed.

Crazy Rambo had become friends with the group's chief soldier, Bloody Charles. Bloody had developed the art of surviving danger and helped the three boys find food in the bush. They would set out at night, grind out mile after mile, then halt briefly before getting back on the trail. Crazy Rambo was scared when he noticed that fatigue had made his calves go dead and his right leg was swollen. Those who complained of swollen legs were killed.

Bloody Charles noticed and asked in a strange, harsher than usual voice, "You look tired Crazy Rambo. Do you want to rest for a while?"

Crazy Rambo felt a knot tighten inside his belly. The thought came suddenly, "Now he's going to kill me!" He heard his own voice answering in a desperately resolute tone, "No, no. I'm fine, I like to walk, let's keep moving."

They were approaching the villages. The road they were on went uphill again. They started up a long path. Straight ahead.

Suddenly the cicadas fell silent as if by magic. They heard shooting.

It was a troop of Ugandan soldiers.

They all threw themselves to the ground.

The bullets whistled over their heads. Hitler Killer, with his neck wrapped in a row of machine gun cartridges, hand grenades strapped to his side, and knife in his sheath, wanted to lunge forward.

Bloody Charles stopped him and said to the group: "There are too many of them!"

They took cover in the thick vegetation. Bloody made everyone camouflage themselves with branches.

During the brief attack, Crazy Rambo was wounded. Terrified, he didn't dare move. He felt paralyzed. Pain spread through every fiber of his body. He felt his legs cave, but he couldn't bring himself to cry. A cloud of angry flies settled on his wounds. Bloody reached over to spread a mixture of herbs and white powder on the sores.

Shortly after, as the drug invaded his blood, the pain disappeared; in fact, he felt strength surge through his whole body. He felt invigorated, ready to walk again. He felt ready to throw himself, eyes closed, right into the bullets hissing by on all sides. He felt invincible. He clenched his teeth and lips tightly.

Commander Dwaka's words, spoken before he left base camp, echoed in his clouded mind: "We are the Army of the Lord Almighty. He protects us with His supernatural power. Do you see this?" he held up the rosary around his neck. "We must recite it a hundred times a day: it is our one and only, our powerful amulet. If you are pure and keep your mouth shut during battle, the bullets will go around you like insects without hitting you. We are the Lord's chosen ones. It is He who commands us to kill, slaughter, rob, and rape the sons and daughters of Evil, members of this criminal government that will not allow us to establish our own constitution based on the Ten Commandments. The Lord revealed this to our *ajwaka*, Her Holiness Lakwena, and cousin of our Supreme Leader Kony. Her Holiness was sent to earth by the Holy Spirit to announce to sinners that they can repent by enlisting to fight against the army of Evil and purify our country with blood: Uganda is the black pearl. Our bombs and bullets are guided by the hand of the Holy Spirit and only strike those who are not worthy to live: traitors and sinners. If we make a mistake in hitting an innocent person, the bullets turn to water in front of his body. You will be killed only if you leave your mouth open. If you keep your mouth open or even half open you will be shot."

Crazy Rambo tightened his lips even more.

The commander's words echoed everywhere: "Ours is a war against war. After a great flood and powerful earthquake, we will bring forth a lasting peace for two hundred years. If you want to be protected against the spells of our enemies you must burn all the *gris-gris*[1] you have on you and swear with the Bible in your right hand that you will never again seek the protection of false idols."

Before finishing his speech, the commander sprinkled them with the water of the Holy Spirit that provided protection against bullets.

"Now go out and fight. If any of you are wounded or killed, it is because you did not keep the Ten Commandments. In any case, at the fall of Kampala, after a short stay in the afterlife, all you true believers will rise again. Upon returning to life, each of you will have a nice house, a big car, and lots of money. Amen."

And they all answered, "Amen!"

By now the unarmed populace of the villages had resigned themselves. They could only breathe freely on Fridays. It was the only day of the week when according to their rules, the Olum could not kill, only whip.

In other villages, at sundown the children would flee from the rebels to the towns of Kitgum, Lira, or Gulu, where they would sleep on verandas, in bus parking lots, or near hospitals. They would arrive as night fell and leave at dawn the next day. They had become a people of darkness, barefoot, silent wanderers, shuttling between home and makeshift shelters. Nearly all of them were children and nearly all of them had bellies swollen with hunger.

In some villages the Acholi women decided to go into mourning in the traditional way: mourning, fasting and refusing to wash or dress until peace returned. Their sacrifices were in vain.

---

1   Charms that are believed to protect the wearer from evil and bring good luck.

When word reached Adak one evening that the rebels were approaching, the neighbor woman told Akwero for the thousandth time to run away to Kitgum as the village children did.

The woman answered, "No! Go, go! I have nothing left to lose. You can't draw water with a basket. They've already taken everything from me. Besides, I'm too old to interest them."

Others considered the warning just one more false alarm.

That night, as the sky crouched over the earth with its cloak of stars and the humid air filled with the deafening croaks of frogs from the nearby pond, the rebels arrived. It was Crazy Rambo's group on the orders of Bloody Charles.

First, they surrounded the village and set fire to the thatch of the outlying huts. The red and yellow flames rose high, illuminating the town as if the sun rose in the middle of the night, casting eerie shadows. They met with no resistance. The over-excited Hitler Killer laughed like a madman, mowing down every life, man or beast, that crossed his path, shouting phrases that he had heard a thousand times and that were now embedded in his brain, "Come out, you unclean rats! Bastards! Degenerates! The Lord's Army has come to save you!"

The village became an inferno, people running in terror, helter-skelter, trying to find safety. Cries of the wounded, human torches spewing from the huts rolling desperately in the dirt. Mutilated bodies, mangled on the ground. In a cacophony of shouts, screams, and crackling weapons, hands and severed heads flew, splattering blood on the walls, on the straw, blood on the ground. An acrid, suffocating smell of smoke and burnt skin. Everything everywhere.

Horrific acts that only human beings know how to inflict on their fellow human beings while the rest of the world dozes indifferent.

Crazy Rambo, followed at a distance by his two friends, was now breaking into the huts, smashing down the doors to flush out the survivors.

Akwero heard voices approaching her hut, angry footsteps, then the sound of machine gun fire drowning out the pleading cries. She sat resigned to her fate, almost relieved to end this torment of life in her discouraged body, her soul shriveled, torn by fear and pain.

A sharp kick threw open the door violently and the shape of a young boy appeared in the entrance. Blinded by the sudden light, Akwero squinted her eyes and stood up proud and determined to meet her destiny. A thought suddenly crossed her mind, "How sad to reach the ancestors without having left any part of me in this life!"

The little boy approached her with wide, expressionless eyes, his mouth contorted into the grimace of an animal about to tear its prey.

Face tense, Akwero's heart stopped beating. They looked at each other.

At first, incredulous, she murmured, "Son." With her arms outstretched towards him, she cried with all her soul, "Son!"

The boy retreated defensively and instinctively pulled the trigger of his Kalashnikov. The echo of the blast rattled the room. The woman screamed again: "Son. Ogaba! My son!" Before she collapsed to the ground, she thought, "What kind of world is this where sons kill their mothers?"

That name, like a bright light piercing the fog, seemed to shake Crazy Rambo.

"Ogaba, Ogaba! That's my name, my real name!" He awoke from his stupor to slowly approach the body of the woman who now lay in a halo of blood. That name recalled smells, flavors, the scent of crunchy sesame, feelings, warm embraces, laughter, school, soccer games with classmates, and swimming in the pond close to home.

Ogaba knelt down next to the woman. Hanging his weapon around his neck, he took Akwero's face in his hands and recognized her. He recognized that sweet, patient look, her lips that were now murmuring, "Oh, good, son . . . You're back . . ." then nothing.

Ogaba began to scream, "Maa! Maa!"

His screams brought Man Eater and Hitler Killer. They found him with his face tear streaked lying on top of the woman's body, sobbing.

Hitler Killer said, "What are you doing Crazy Rambo? Are you insane? Let's go!"

"Let's go, Crazy!" repeated Man Eater.

Ogaba looked up and stated in a quiet, firm voice: "My name is not Crazy Rambo. My name is Ogaba. My name is Ogaba and this is my mother. This woman is my mother. I killed her. This is maa. My name is Ogaba."

He saw his companions look at each other. Ogaba clung to the woman and breathed in her scent deeply: he knew what was going to happen.

THE INVISIBLE HAND

Selì joined his Senegalese friend at the home of Japanese acquaintances in one of those densely populated neighborhoods just outside the city.

They went directly down to the basement workshop jittering with people assembling small plastic objects. Kebe was certainly tall, but in the midst of the workers he seemed like Gulliver among the Lilliputians. When he and Selì had walked in, they were greeted by the workers' momentary silence before everyone went right back to work, some with their heads down and others carrying the goods from one bench to another. Kebe was at ease as usual, but Selì felt out of place.

Apropos of nothing, Kebe suggested dancing to show his friend a bit of Japanese tradition. His invitation was met with giggles and shouts of enthusiasm. In no time at all, the workshop was transformed as if by magic into a stage where girls with shy smiles began to dance with tiny steps. They performed measured movements to the sound of a strange, inexplicable music, like a cascade of water drops tinkling on a zinc roof. An intoxicating scent of peach blossoms wafted through the air. Everything seemed unreal and dream-like.

Selì felt guilty when he saw the work boxes stacked up and abandoned in a corner. The workers had, out of a sense of hospitality perhaps, sacrificed some of their earnings, because if Selì understood it, they were paid according to the quantity of widgets processed. Yet here they were joyful and serene. He could not understand the relationship between them and Kebe, but certainly there was mutual respect and esteem, maybe even friendship.

Lost in his thoughts, Selì hadn't noticed the paper screen until Kebe and one of the workers moved behind it, transformed suddenly into shadow puppets. The discussion seemed very animated but ended immediately with one of the Senegalese's thunderous laughs and then they both leaned forward in an exaggerated manner with hands mockingly clasped together around their bellies, concluding their conference with pats on the back.

Swinging his arms, Kebe reached Selì in two strides, "Tonight you are my special guest at a surprise party!"

"Surprise party? A Japanese surprise party?"

"Yes."

"But . . ."

"No buts, trust your Kebe! Have I ever deceived you?"

"No but . . ."

"Just do as I say and you'll see that everything will be fine."

When evening came, Kebe took Selì back to the same neighborhood. The lights of the night softened the impersonal landscape of the day's harsh concrete cathedrals. Now shrouded in twilight, they transformed into gigantic towers with their windows lit up like stars strung about the Milky Way. The two friends entered the garden of an apartment building. The place was decorated with oil lamps placed across the grounds, illuminating everything with a soft light: they looked like so many fireflies playing hide and seek.

Kebe whispered in his friend's ear, "Don't be surprised by anything, just follow your instincts, and use the sweetest and most poetic language you can find."

"What?"

His question remained unanswered, because Kebe disappeared like a ghost into a crowd, lost amongst the other whispering guests. All seemed aimed towards the gazebo planted in the middle of the garden. Selì tried to follow behind, but he was stopped by a powerfully built Japanese man who blocked his way. It was the same man Kebe had been whispering with behind the screen. In front of Selì, this man held out a strange object: a small porcelain vase adorned with origami. Amazed and frightened, Selì regarded the object suspiciously, as if it were a bomb or who knows what kind of talisman.

The man placed the object in Selì's hand and before a word could be exchanged, the man too disappeared into the crowd. In his disorientation, Selì's trembling fingers let slip the object which promptly shattered to pieces, wetting the ground with the yellowish liquid it contained. When Selì looked up again, he found himself in front of a woman who seemed to have emerged magically from the vase; she was wrapped in a silk kimono of the same colors as the origami decorations. He felt his heart quiver like butterfly wings as he met her intense gaze. Again, he smelled the pungent scent of peach blossoms in the air. Her deep black hair was gathered at the top of her head, and held in place by a pink bow. Her half-opened lips, moist as the petals of a pale flower pearled with morning dew, murmured: "Come!"

Her cool, soft fingers imprisoned his, dragging him toward the gazebo.

Selì wanted to speak, to ask, to understand. He opened his mouth to ask, "Who are you? What's going on?" but no sound escaped.

He was overcome by a single, incredible, and inexplicable certainty: next to him was the most beautiful woman he had ever seen, the love of his life, the one he had always dreamed about. Selì ardently desired this woman. He wanted her for himself: he would have faced any danger for her. He was ready to lose his soul for her.

With a light step, she led him to sit on a red sofa amid the other guests already seated. As they took their place, all fell silent for a moment that seemed like an eternity.

The powerfully built Japanese man rose from his cushion with surprising agility. He bowed three times before them, then turned to Selì and asked, pointing at the young woman: "Honorable guest, is she to your liking?"

Selì turned towards her as if to reassure himself that he was not dreaming and refrained from answering abruptly, "How could she not be?" Then he remembered Kebe's mysterious advice.

Selì felt the gaze of everyone present clutching at him. The girl squeezed his fingers gently and a smile lit up her face. He answered: "Her face floods me with tenderness, her gaze caresses my soul and makes my heart languish in a lemon-flavored whirlpool."

The man, seemingly satisfied by his answer, bowed three more times, and gathering his golden kimono around his body returned to sit with a majestic gesture, amidst the applause of the guests.

Selì turned, delighted, towards the young girl. He wanted to talk to her, to at least know her name, but she did not allow him to do so, placing her perfumed index finger on his lips to invite him to silence. At that precise moment, the man in the golden kimono stood up again, unsheathing, with an expert hand, a long and threatening shiny sword. Terrified and lightning fast, Selì stood up as if bitten by a tarantula and assumed a defensive stance.

His gesture was greeted by a general "Oh!" of disapproval and disappointment.

The Japanese man angrily sheathed his weapon, turned, and left.

Astonished Selì looked around. In a sepulchral silence, as in a nightmare, everyone got up and, without giving him a glance, walked like shadows to the exit.

The girl let go of his hand and a bitter tear slipped silently down her cheek: "You have offended and angered my father. Your soul is not ready for the sacrifice of love: he cannot consent to our union!"

Her voice was imbued with sadness.

Selì stretched out his hands towards her, but she too vanished.

He woke up sweating in his bed: it had all been a dream.

He felt a mixture of relief and disquiet. Rolling over, he picked up the pages of the newspaper he was reading before falling asleep and his eyes caught a headline: "Monsignor Milingo, the well-known African bishop and exorcist-singer marries a Korean woman in a collective ceremony."

"What a mysterious path guides the meanderings of the human mind!" thought Selì as his cell phone played the first notes of Beethoven's fifth symphony for the third time.

"Hello!"

"Hi Selì!"

"Oh! Hello Kebe! It's you! Listen, you know . . ."

"Listen . . . I'm in a hurry. I called to see about a party tonight. Do you want to go?"

"A party?"

"Yes! A surprise party."

"I bet it's with your Japanese friends!"

"Yes, but how did you know?"

The invisible hand that weaves the textures of our lives has so many threads in its loom.

"So are you coming?"

". . . ?"

BEATS

And the serpent said unto the woman, Ye shall not surely die:
For God doth know that in the day ye eat thereof,
then your eyes shall be opened,
and ye shall be as gods, knowing good and evil.

GENESIS 3:4-5

For the past thirty days, every time I wake up it's worse. Out of the corner of my eye I can see the impression Daniela's body left on my sheets. I get out of bed and go to the bathroom. The crystal lights on the wall remind me: January 10, 2054, appointment with Prof. Dolly, 9 am. The bathroom walls echo back the image of a man with dark skin, no longer handsome. Hair that is growing too gray forms a crown around my nascent baldness. I note in passing the double chin and the crows-feet at the corners of my eyes. I avoid looking at the triple roll around my middle that I wear like a life preserver; I see it more like an apron that I persist on calling "love handles." Looking at myself, I feel a wave of sadness from the bottom of my soul: deep down, I've come to love this body. Once upon a time, Daniela had liked it, too. It's been a month since I've seen her; I feel her absence.

As if waving away a fly, I rubbed my right hand over my face to dislodge the memories that tore at my soul. I had to admit that, despite everything, I was still in love with her. I got dressed slowly. My appointment with Dr. Dolly wasn't for another hour. For the love of Dany, I'm ready to do anything.

I had time to chew and swallow two sticks of chocolate-croissant-flavored gum before jumping into the glass elevator down from the 120th floor. I've never been able to stand heights. My knees even go weak on an escalator. I look up at the tiny square of gray sky that covers the space between the two skyscrapers. The stale, acidic, heavy air of the city crowds into the elevator as soon as it hits the ground. Before merging into the hurrying crowd, I quickly insert air filters into my nostrils. When I arrive at Dr. Dolly's office he greets me with, "So, you old wreck, have you finally made up your mind?"

I remain silent. He takes that for an answer.

Thoughts perch in my brain like notes along a musical staff. As I follow the doctor, I drop the pitch of my thoughts a semitone so as to only hear my heart. My heart pulses to a hip hop medley, just like every time I embrace Dany, even just the thought of her . . .

In the operating room, someone undresses me. I'm hot. Nurse Someone has blonde hair peeking out from under her blue cap, framing a pretty little face with hazel eyes that fix on me pitilessly. In her half-indifferent, half-judgmental gaze I can read – not without some pain – the full extent of my physical decay which no doubt due to its severity, makes her glance downwards. I'm sure she compares my family jewels to her lover's; she probably jealously guards those in his underwear and only reveals them under the sheets in her own alcove. My macho African pride does a couple of backflips and sets off a few fireworks when I notice a brief, almost imperceptible flick of her eyelids, confirming the myth about size that has run through the collective imagination of Whites for centuries. My Daniela lost any such illusions long ago: my proboscis-shaped appendage doesn't assume the happiness-ecstasy position as spontaneously or often as I would like.

"Ah, the irreparable insult of the passing years!"

As I look at myself, I suddenly see that I really am old, decrepit, senile. The idea of growing old no longer fills me with the peace and happiness.

I had always thought of old age as a goal, an achievement. When I died, I wanted to be like "a library that burned down." I'd definitely made a bad choice of where to grow old and die. Even worse, where to be born. I lived out my childhood weighed down by hauling buckets of water and loads of wood, with my neck twisted up and my bare feet burned on the hot sand, with a Nestlé box instead of a soccer ball because Santa Claus must have lost his bearings when he crossed the Mediterranean Sea. His reindeer and sleigh must have run aground in the sand in the dunes of the Ténéré. Or maybe when he was flying over our scorched savannah lands, the white-bearded old man had turned his sleigh around because looking across the horizon, he didn't see any chimneys, just the unfortunate confusion of giant termite mounds. His reindeer, all sweaty, smelly, and depressed by the heat and humidity of the place, might have gone on strike, then outvoted Father Christmas at the negotiating table over the labor conflict; their demands would undermine economic stability and send the GDP plummeting from Scylla to Charybdis. All that is to say, where I grew up, we'd never seen Santa's snowy beard appear even on the distant horizon of our childhood wishes. We couldn't even hang our gift-filled dreams along the fireplace or on the beautiful-best-of-the-forest-Christmas-tree for the simple reason that we didn't have fireplaces or Christmas trees. Where I grew up, in the land of Ham's descendants, we had only the great-baobab-tree-of-*palabre*,[1] as vast as wisdom itself, so big that one man alone couldn't possibly reach his arms around it. Day and night under this tree, our elders, the rightful guardians of accepted wisdom, would salivate toothless words, tinged with cola nuts. Our childhood dreams, flying on the iron bird to reach Toyland, caught in the branches of the *filao*[2] where they ripened without ever blooming like the vermillion red flowers of the bougainvilleas that fenced the walls of our house. For fun we'd had to make do chasing after the exhaust pipes of the sputtering Citroën DSs that we'd christened "ground planes."

On several occasions, I had complained to Daniela – my colorless better half – at the slightest squeaking of the chain, the same chain that united us for eight years of life together, during which we'd never thought it useful to get married officially.

---

1 From French, an expression to indicate the assembly place in regions across Africa where issues concerning the community are discussed.

2 A tree similar to the cluster pine used in Africa to protect houses from dust and unwanted visitors.

I wanted my voice to be sharp and wounding: "You can't understand me because you've always lived in luxury!"

"Oh, you and your poor Black child routine!"

"Don't make fun of me . . . you pink child!"

She withdrew into one of those self-righteous silences, the kind that pretends to hang the white flag of surrender on the tip of her lips to avoid getting involved in my visceral rants that have no real beginning or end. A real diatribe in true pale-face style. Living with Whites, I learned from them and perfected the "art of winning without being right."

I believed it was a good idea to insist, though my tone was indignant, vindictive: "It's immoral! Santa Claus brings gifts to children who are already greedy and spoiled!"

She pretended to relent by purring: "You're right, darling. Life has been so unfair to you. But do you know what the real problem is, my dear?

"No . . . Enlighten me!"

"At your age, you still believe in Santa Claus!"

She joined the sentence with her throaty laugh that sent chills under my skin and woke up my hormones.

She knew it and came to hug me. I would pretend to resist and we would laugh. I would try to have the last word but she knew my Achilles heel. Her voracious mouth devoured mine, she filled my ears with a flow of "I love yous," poured out lavishly. I surrendered and our hands blindly found the usual grooves of our mountains and valleys, our wells and springs, where we would drink from caresses to quench our thirst for tenderness. Later, while I was wiping away the sweat that beaded her temple, and she mine, I returned indirectly to the subject.

"I didn't choose very well where to be born, and even worse where to grow old."

"I'm only afraid of growing old . . ."

"Why? Every season has its fruits. Old age is beautiful!"

"Old age, my foot! After thirty, every day you wake up and feel a pain somewhere, your skin becomes flabby, your boobs sag, cellulite turns your hips into orange peels, your teeth rot and fall out. You choke at the slightest strain and your joints creak. It's horrible! Old people smell of urine, illness, and sweat! I don't want to get old."

"Baby, you're talking like a product of your culture!"

"Well, the wise African sage has spoken!"

"It's just your society."

"It's been your society, too, for the last half a century!"

"Your culture only sees a man as the metaphorical image of a machine. Doctors divide up our bodies like spare car parts. The hepatologist is only concerned with my liver, the cardiologist with my heart."

"And the gastroenterologist only with your guts . . . "

"That's how it is! And if some part of the body's engine stops working, a bolt is removed here, a screw is tightened there. Little by little the body-machine loses all its mystery along with the revolution of optical fibers: they penetrate everywhere with their ultrasounds, CT scans, MRIs, and all their devilish arts."

"That's called progress, old man!

"I don't give a damn about this so-called progress if it doesn't see me as a whole entity. I'm not just a body!"

"What else?"

"Gosh, I don't know: I also have a spirit, feelings, maybe even a soul . . . "

"My dear, what planet are you on? We left that era behind a century ago. From the body-machine we moved to the body-computer to create the bionic man with all possible and conceivable forms of prosthesis. If you have a lopsided hip they can fix it in a flash with a prosthesis. If your heart doesn't pump anymore, they can replace it, if your penis droops from gravity, they will straighten it right back up..."

"It's true."

"And we're not done yet! You can't stop progress! Humans can become eternal!"

"Yes, if man wants to replace his creator! But no! Dany, no! I want to grow old!"

"Not me! As soon as I feel old, I'll go to Dr. Dolly and have myself cloned!"

"Do what?"

"Clone myself!"

"Clone yourself? Are you serious?"

Her message couldn't have been any clearer: "Old man, it's time to go get cloned!

I cursed myself for becoming involved with a woman twenty years younger than me. Be cloned! I'd always been terrified by the idea of duplicating, of photocopying a human being.

The human cloning bill was the first to use the scratch-off lotto card voting system; when exiting the polling station, those who had voted were offered the opportunity to place a free bet on the final result, scratching in a system of two columns the exact percentage of the presumed "yes" and "no" votes. The winners shared the prize of four billion euros. For the referendum on cloning, voter turnout was almost ninety percent.

Medical science had made giant strides since the failed experiments of Dr. Vieri Senantinoro. Now making a "copy," as it was called, had become a trend; cloning was strongly supported by economic globalization for it promised a panacea for the problems of falling birthrates and the need for providing pensions. Essentially, thanks to replication, old people became young again, so they could efficiently return to work, drooling to continue filling the social security coffers with their taxable contributions. However, competition in the global market was fierce and increasingly intensified the generational conflicts between the OYs (Old-Youngs) and the YY s (Young-Youngs) who were left grumbling about flexible unemployment. The new duplication method developed by Dr. Dolly, although still imperfect, allowed the retention of memory and experience, which gave the OYs an advantage. Citing these developments, Dany insisted her value, her dignity as a human being was not linked to the uniqueness of her genes but to the uniqueness of her experience and personal history, which according to her, were more important than her biological reality.

In all this debate I would have lost my Latin and Greek, if only I had studied them. To me, a person was a whole entity, both in biology and experience, and to me, cloning seemed to violate natural laws. My culture had taught me to accept life as a gift, old age as a privilege, and death as inevitable in order to cross over to the other side of the river into the land of the ancestors, even if you can't swim. But here in Euroland, we TOs (True Olds) were definitely viewed like archaeological relics.

Dany and I went back and forth on this a thousand times. Each time we ended up back to the starting point, each of us returning a little groggy to our respective corners without throwing in the towel. The conversation irritated us like a fishbone between our teeth. And each time one of our friends became a "copy," the arguments became more frequent and the tone less civil.

She never missed an opportunity to point out my physical decline. With an ultra-wide fisheye zoom, she'd take close-ups of the evidence that she seasoned with commentary and subtext. She'd launch an offensive with an innocent voice and phrases that were intended to sound innocuous: "Old man, you're neglecting yourself," "You should eat a little less at your age and watch your figure," "You know, honey, I'm saying this for your own good," and finally hit me with the delightful "You know, at your age . . ."

I have to admit that yes, I'd lost the habit of caring for my body the way I once did.

With the arrival of every summer, I'd imagine myself as I was when I was young, lying on a deserted beach of fine sand, cradled by the waves of the sea, under the admiring gazes of young and old sirens enraptured before my sculpted body. Then, inevitably every evening, I gorged myself on angry resolutions against my number one enemy, "fat," the plump product accumulated during those abundant winter meals.

"Starting tomorrow, I'll park my car further away to take a few more steps, I won't take the elevator but only the stairs, and above all I'll stop smoking." "Starting tomorrow," I promised myself, "I'll skip breakfast to go jogging." "Starting tomorrow, I'll only eat fruit or vegetables at noon and in the evening just a little soup, then I'll exercise for two hours, I'll go bike riding, then have a nice shower before going to bed." Always "starting tomorrow."

After that came nightmarish nights filled with stomach cramps and dreams of ravenous green mice attacking Mount Gruyere. Every year when summer approached, I would go to my closet and nostalgically contemplate my beautiful shirts that I could only button by holding my breath. I would peek with hope at my old pants that clung to my thighs and stubbornly stayed open at the waistband, ones that I had saved for "when I get back in shape." "Tomorrow" I would regain the physique that I'd been proud of and that I was sure had won Daniela over at first sight.

Inevitably, at breakfast the next day, I forgot all about it while I buttered toast before spreading on a generous layer of jam to satisfy my atavistic hunger. The flesh is weak and the fat is hard to melt! Even back then, the cult of the model body was in vogue: there were no more children with crooked teeth or flat feet. I used to denounce the risks of this image, this idolatry of the perfect body that led to pathological conditions like bulimia and anorexia.

Daniela did not give up her body fetish. She spent hours in the gym immolating fatigue and sweat on the altar of the gods of fitness, step workout and bodybuilding. She had tattoos and piercings on every square meter of her skin.

I wanted to get in my shots where I could: "I think you once called us savages because we used to do these same things!"

She shrugged her shoulders indifferently. By dint of her phobia of aging, a real paranoia, she finally convincing me to go and meet her hero: the famous Dr. Dolly. After all, a visit was not a promise and a promise is nothing more than a "yes" made in the future tense.

He was a man of indefinite age with strange gray eyes that mesmerized you and seemed to pierce and desiccate your soul. Dr. Dolly, a scientist of world renown, had developed the famous Nuclear Cloning Transfer method that he took upon himself to explain to me: "The cloning method is very simple. We take an egg cell from the HOB (human ova bank) and a cell from your skin. We empty the egg cell of its original DNA. We will then fill the egg cell with nuclear extracts of your epidermal cell. The new ovum thus obtained will be nested in the Uterotronic-Velox, a growth accelerator, which in the space of three days will reproduce you exactly as you are, or decide at what age to regenerate you."

I stopped breathing: "It's like science fiction!"

When I caught my breath, a question came out: "What do I become?"

"You are always you. Your DNA preserves everything about you, even your memory."

"Yes, I know, but me, I mean my old body, what do you do with it?"

"Initially, it will be put in hibernation while we wait to see the final result. If all goes well, the old model will be cremated; if you want, you can keep the ashes as a souvenir."

"That's terrible!"

Dany was over the moon: "This is fabulous! It's progress!"

"Progress, progress, progress—that's the only word you say, but that progress there gives me the willies. I get knots in the pit of my stomach."

Silence. Then tortuous doubt: "And what if it doesn't work? What if it turns me into a monster?"

"There are no risks. On the contrary, duplication opens the door to human improvement, because in a certain sense you can develop the best parts of yourself."

She irritated me.

"This is insane. Who can say what the best part of someone is, who sets the standard for what kind of person is best, what is the best part of human nature?"

"No, this is wonderful! One day we will be able to build a perfect human, predict diseases and prevent them."

"Can you imagine the benefits for mankind?" Daniela insisted.

Questions, thorny like cacti, crystallized into thoughts that clung to my brain:

"What will be the risks to future generations? We have already seen the damage that GMOs have brought. Of course, GMOs have made it possible to overcome world hunger, but at what cost? We have witnessed a sudden and inexplicable growth of strange allergies in children, widespread sterility in couples, an increase in cancerous diseases, plus the pervasive depression of the immune system."

My voice overheats to unconvincingly enunciate: "No! The day you start building humans who are better than others, our whole principle of equality, of equal opportunities among human beings will go straight to hell!"

Astonished silence.

I continued, "In a way, cloning is a form of violence towards the foundation of life: adventure. What sense would this life have without the marvel, the sense of wonder that adds spice to life? Isn't existence also this continuous, surprising and amazing discovery of oneself and one's destiny? Where would my freedom go without my personal history? Life would be sad without events, without surprises!"

At my refusal, Dany looked straight through me, as if I was transparent, then shrugged and left the office without a word. I hadn't seen her since.

All this happened a month ago.

"Dogs bark . . . a trailer passes by."

I open my eyes and my gaze meets that of Nurse Someone. I immediately recognize her. She smiles at me and murmurs: "Welcome, you are back among the living! Here are your clothes!"

I feel fit . . . I feel young. Now I am a copy.

Anxiety creeps into me. I lift the sheet, I look at my naked body: I'm at least twenty years younger and it shows! I catch Nurse Someone's eye and her face turns bright red before she stammers: "I'll ca—, I'll call Dr. Dolly."

Dr. Dolly enters just as I finish dressing.

He answers my questioning look: "Everything is fine! I told your companion, just as you asked: she's outside waiting for you."

Suddenly I'm out of the room. I recognize Dany's silhouette in the corridor. I walk, then run towards her. She comes towards me and we embrace, but I cannot find the intoxication of her scent. She pulls me close and covers my face and then my lips with kisses. I no longer recognize the taste. I look into her eyes and realize that it's really her, but my heart no longer beats as it once did, no boom bap. My heart thumps but only like the freaking muscle it is, period! I feel nothing else! I feel lost. I feel dizzy. I look around for something to grab onto.

Behind Daniela, I see Nurse Someone. She waves her fingers and winks, then turns and walks away. My eyes follow the dance of her shapely curves moving in rhythm and suddenly my heart muscle begins to swing to that beat.

MADIBA

> A winner is a dreamer
> who has not surrendered.
>
> NELSON MANDELA

"But, she's white!" or more often, "She's not black!" These were the expected and inevitable expressions and exclamations, usually accompanied by widened eyes whenever Giorgia introduced me as her "African friend" or "South African friend." Yes, I am South African, proudly South African! My name is — or rather, I think it's more accurate to say that others call me — Sandra Berrisi. Come to think of it, no one "calls themselves" unless they're crazy; it's others who call us.

I am South African, of Italian origin; my grandfather arrived in the region then called Transvaal in 1948 (now Mpumalanga), at the end of the Second World War, when there were rumors that the communists were going to take over Italy and confiscate property from the wealthy and everyone else who had collaborated with the fascist regime. My grandfather was forty-five years old when he founded a small textile industry in the vicinity of Standerton with his friends and his savings. My father moved to the Kwazulu Natal region after his marriage to *la mamma*, who was originally from Tuscany. That was just after the victory of the National Party[1] which established the harsh law of apartheid. I was born in Durban. I've always lived in South Africa, except for some vacations spent in Italy with relatives. I've always considered myself South African.

---

1 The National Party (Nasionale Party in Afrikaans, NP) is a South African political party founded in 1914 and dissolved in 2005. The National Party was the political expression of Afrikaans nationalism in the 20th century, nostalgic for the independence of the Boer republics.

I remember the astonished looks of my cousin Annamaria's friends during the summer vacations in Italy. Annamaria, like Giorgia, would introduce me with a joking smile, "My cousin Sandra," and then she would add with a hint of wickedness, "She's . . . South African."

And then, always came the questioning looks: How? She's white! Uh, a white South African? And then, inevitable curiosity that followed in the form of accusing looks that came with the word "apartheid." Associations and ideas hung on that word, of course, like the song "Pata Pata"[2] and the image of Nelson Mandela.[3]

God, how I hated that name! Nelson Mandela: a man I didn't even know and never wanted to know but who poisoned my life. I was one year old when he was sentenced to life in prison on Robben Island, off the coast of Capetown. Later, after the Soweto massacre and Steve Biko's death, when I was about thirteen, I asked my grandfather about Mandela and he said: "That *kaffir*[4] is a dangerous criminal. He's a terrorist, a communist who only wants to kill all of us Whites and take our wealth and land. He's the one who created the *Umkhonto we Sizwe*; that means 'the spear of the nation.' Their anthem swears that it wants to kill all *ama bhulu*, all the Whites, and take our place! They blew up bridges and police stations. They raped our women! Good thing he's in jail!"

---

2   "Pata Pata" is a song by South African singer Miriam Makeba (1932-2008), also known by the pseudonym of Mama Africa. The song, written in the Xhosa language, is about a traditional South African dance whose meaning is "touch touch."

On the night she died, Miriam Makeba performed "Pata Pata" just before she collapsed on stage in Italy.

3   Nelson Mandela was the first president of South Africa from 1994 to 1999. For twenty-seven years, he was imprisoned for his role in leading anti-apartheid movements. His release from prison, amid growing internal and international pressures, sparked negotiations to end the anti-democratic government. Known popularly by his Thembu clan name Madiba, Mandela won the Nobel Peace Prize in 1993 for his efforts to dismantle apartheid and its legacy in South Africa.

4   A racial term and ethnic slur used to refer to black Africans in South Africa.

For me, though, Nelson Mandela remained just a name until one summer day when I met Jerry. I'd come to spend the summer in Italy and we were with my cousin Annamaria and other friends at a party in the disco *Bandieragialla* in Rimini, the capital of the Romagna Riviera. Roberta, one of those committed #flap[5] type of people, introduced us that night with a hint of controversy in her voice, "Sandra, a South African, this is Jerry . . . South African!" My first thought was, "Oh, my God, he's so black!"

Jerry was really black! Of course, as a South African, I knew Black people, I'd lived among them since I was a child, but this was the first time I'd really seen one so close that I could smell his breath. True, our old Xhosa housekeeper had lived with us forever; she'd seen the birth of my older sister and me, but she was a fixture, part of the background in the house, and I'd never looked at her the way I did Jerry that night. I remember that once when we were little, *la mamma* let us play with our cook's children, against my father's wishes, because she didn't share his apartheid ideas. Soon the neighbors reported us to the police, who came to tell us that if we wanted to live like those under communism, we could leave at any time.

I remember that the police came twice more to harass my mother because she was paying her servants too much. The neighbors caught on when they noticed the servants were able to afford such luxury items as bicycles.

On another occasion, they came to order us to destroy the roof that made our house adjoin the Blacks' outbuilding, because the law forbade Whites and Blacks to sleep under the same roof.

It was after this episode, which was followed by intimidation and more or less veiled threats, that *la mamma* taught us to observe and maintain what she christened "the status quo." I learned that respecting it also avoided causing serious trouble for the Blacks. Ever tenacious, my mother persisted in trying to help them in other ways, either by paying for part of their children's school fees, books, and notebooks or by trying to find help for their health problems.

---

5   #freeloveandprotest.

The racial separation was clearly defined: from park benches to seats on the bus, bathrooms, and even stores. In the beginning, my mother went to the butcher's through the door for Whites and bought meat for our servants as well. The Blacks often couldn't afford to buy prime cuts, so when they went to the butcher, on their side, of course, they would buy the organ meats: tripe, liver, heart, kidneys, lungs, which the Whites didn't like, and as soon as White customers arrived on the other side, the butcher would leave quickly to serve them.

We were told that the *kaffir* were inferior and were separated from us by divine will, just as God separates the ducks from the sparrows, and that it was only fitting to institute the requirement of permits to better manage the divine order. The Blacks could move around in the city center from Monday to Friday until nightfall and could travel to the outskirts of the city, the townships, where they could drink cheap kafir beer only on Friday, which they got drunk on to numb their bad thoughts, their unspoken desires. On weekends, the city center was so wonderful and safe. That was the status quo. I was born into it and for us, it was normal, or almost.

Now I see it more clearly. Before, I was completely confused, my head, my heart. Well, I must give some order to my thoughts.

It's strange how we live with our convictions, our certainties, and after an event or an encounter, all of a sudden, everything collapses. It was like regaining your sight after years of blindness. My meeting with Jerry was just such a life-changing experience.

I remember we sat in a corner of the club, but the volume of the music didn't allow us to talk, and at first, I was glad. It was a relief from the tedium of having to answer the usual series of questions about apartheid, whether or not it was right for four million people to deny the right to speak and vote to more than twenty million people simply because they have black skin. My enjoyment though was short-lived. It was Annamaria who suggested the fateful idea, "Come on! Shall we go have a *mangi e bevi*[6] at Pino's?"

I must confess that I could never resist such an invitation: sweets are one of my weaknesses and since I make a point of giving in to

---

6 An ice cream dessert with seasonal fruits (melon, kiwi, watermelon) and berries.

all my weaknesses, any opportunity to cheat on my diet is a good opportunity.

On the terrace at Pino's, the sea breeze was ruffling our hair and coating our lips with a film of salt spray. Then the #flap Roberta, with a rather accusatory and cutting tone, introduced me to Jerry—a South African political refugee, persecuted at home because of apartheid, who escaped from forced labor in the Transvaal mines. He'd lost his father and his seven-year-old daughter in the racial clashes. The pain had torn his soul apart and rage had possessed him like a demon. For fear of committing the irreparable, he had fled, leaving his young wife and two other sons behind while he sought a better life for them all. In short, Jerry, like so many others, attracted by the mirage of Europe and freedom, was working "under the table" harvesting tomatoes in the countryside, in the province of Caserta, *camorra* territory. The working conditions were harsh; men were forced to live in shacks, isolated, due to the hostility of locals. Jerry was passing through Rimini at the invitation of an association for the defense of immigrants, which had asked him to speak out about their working conditions, to raise awareness, and to call for support.

The province of Caserta produced almost a million tons of tomatoes. The red gold, however, had to be harvested in a period of two months: July and August. With such a narrow window, there was work for thousands of people, condensed into the two months when most Italians vacationed. There was the possibility of earning a good living by working hard in these two months, even for undocumented migrants, insulated as they were by the general climate of illegality and only sporadic controls by the police.

As was easily foreseeable, these conditions attracted thousands of young immigrants from North African countries. In two months, working from dawn to dusk, up to fifteen hours a day, they could accumulate savings that allowed them to survive and also provide for the needs of their families back home. These day laborers quickly became easy prey for the landowners, and very quickly the rumors about cheap available labor ran through the fields, among the farmers, until they reached the ears of those who "organized" the trips of hope.

Of course, the fact that the *camorra* reigns sovereign in these areas facilitates this illegal labor market. As a result, the pay, the working conditions, the basic hygiene, and above all the safety of the workers were certainly far from the best.

Roberta observed, "Jerry, you know, you're really unlucky; you went from one form of slavery to another."

"At least here I can justify it to myself because I am a foreigner and I have a choice."

An awkward silence arose; the ice cream lost its taste, I could feel everyone's glares like needles perforating my skin. They were all waiting for me to say something. I didn't know what to say; faced with my painful silence, Jerry went on the offensive: "I can't understand!"

"Understand what?" I went hard on the defense.

"Deep down, you had an advantage over others your age, you came regularly to Italy, and you heard that here everyone was against apartheid, and you also saw Black people living here normally."

"It's true that what first shocked me in Italy was to see White people doing heavy labor and all the dirty jobs that only Black people do in our country. Here in Italy, Blacks are a minority; back home, there are many more of them; they used to scare us and they still do."

After a brief silence: "And you never doubted that it was unjust, you who are believer, a Christian, and moreover a Catholic?"

"My God, Jerry, what do you want me to say? The priest told us that it was normal, that it was God who wanted it that way, that the fingers on a hand are not equal, that Black people live well like that and that's why they're always cheerful and smiling."

"#flap" judged me, condemned me, and machine-gunned me mercilessly, "What nonsense, Sandra! How could you believe such drivel?"

"It's easy for you to say that from here, but for us who were living it, it's different. It's human nature to find convenient anything that brings us privilege, and I admit that it was convenient. Besides, if you had any doubts, all you had to do was to sit down, silence your conscience and everything would go back to the way it was. We all like our privileges and we are all ready to sacrifice anything to preserve them. That was the status quo!"

Jerry knew well that South Africans were classified into four racial groups from top to bottom: Whites, Indians, Africans, and at the bottom the "colored" mulattoes, often the result of rape. The protester-heroine, the unblemished Roberta, returned to the attack. "That's too easy! That's the same excuse many used to deny the Holocaust." Jerry listened, eyes half-closed.

"Listen to me, little miss know-it-all, in all societies, there are inconsistencies, values, as well as professed values. You're so ready to judge others, but for example, do you actually believe that two or three women are really happy to share the same man? Without being jealous?"

"Yes, but . . . this is tradition!"

"Tradition, the status quo . . . call it what you will, it's all the same!"

Jerry opened his eyes and with an anxious voice, asked, "Listen, Sandra: I understand what you mean about the habit and the excuse of tradition; for example, there are African countries where they still barbarically circumcise young girls and I hear people here in Italy complacently justifying that with the relativistic argument that 'It's just their culture!' But you're young, you have a university education, you're an intellectual, you cannot fail to understand! Surely you've read authors like Coetzee and Gordimer, they all condemned apartheid!"

"Those books were practically impossible to find. They were banned!"

Roberta, with her forked tongue, never missed a chance to layer it on, "Give me a break! There's nothing more appealing than the forbidden!"

I kept asking myself why everyone wanted me to answer for the sins of apartheid. Basically, I was only eighteen or nineteen years old when Umkhonto resumed its campaign of bombing and sabotaging power stations, communication centers, and police stations. It was at this time that I secretly read *My Traitor's Heart* by Rian Malan, the nephew of the apartheid ideologue. That book impressed me, asked me questions, but I had no one to discuss them with, cut off from developing answers. At the university, we talked secretly about the protests in the country and in the rest of the world, about the sports boycotts, the concerts, and especially about the economic embargo. Some white students began to openly criticize the government, and Nelson Mandela had already managed to get himself moved from Robben Island to Pollsmoor on the mainland. Despite this gesture of goodwill, the violence came to a head and the government imposed a state of emergency. We were all scared.

"Sandra, you have to understand that after so many years in prison, after losing his friends in the struggle, giving up a normal life . . . Mandela cannot give up."

"Give up wanting to kill us all to take over?"

"No, the old man doesn't want to kill you. That's the propaganda of those in power. The old man doesn't want to give up his beliefs and he's willing to die for them. Mandela's political equation is simple: in our country, power has kidnapped freedom, so the only way to regain freedom for our people is to take power."

"With force?"

"No, and no, again! Mandela says, 'I have cultivated the ideal of a free and democratic society in which all can live together in harmony, with equal opportunities. That is an ideal I hope to live for . . .' Mandela simply proposes democracy: one man, one vote in free elections."

"Jerry, do you really think that's possible back home?"

"Change must come and it doesn't depend solely on the Whites wanting it. Living together equitably involves more than one person and both must want it. The South Africa we dream of will not be offered to us like a pretty cake on a golden platter. Life has taught me that the things that are given to us as gifts can be taken away just as easily, but the things that we've sacrificed for, that we've gritted our teeth to achieve, cannot be snatched away from us so easily; because we fought for them, and we'll fight tenaciously to keep them. We Black South Africans need to stop crying about ourselves if we are to overcome our complexes."

Jerry went on to explain that in order to win and take power, we didn't need to proclaim that "Black is beautiful!"

"'Black is beautiful! Black is beautiful don't you know!' said the American Negros, sorry, the 'Afro-Americans' of the Black Power movement that developed in the sixties in the United States. No one is interested anymore in hearing that 'black is beautiful.' Is it really true that 'black is beautiful'? If it's true, then what need is there to assert it, sometimes at the top of our lungs? Wole Soyinka already gave his answer: 'The tiger does not proclaim its *tigritude*, it pounces on its prey and devours it.'"

Jerry went on, "It seems that the sons of Ham carry their pigmentation like a curse, a shame for which they must atone. They have remained slaves to the Dominant Power, like 'those who invented neither gunpowder nor the compass,' content to be 'dark toys at the carnival of others,' and still feel the need to come to terms with their woeful color. Black is the color of darkness, of the soul doomed to hell. Blinding white is the light which, in itself, contains in prism all the colors of the rainbow. Black is the hunger with which my race has been flirting for centuries, despite having slaved in the cotton fields that made the 'northern worlds' rich, those who devastated immense forests of human ebony by chaining them in the holds of their ships. Today, as we pay the debts incurred by others, we wonder when humanity will pay its debt to Mother Africa—the debt to which she never agreed—for raping and exploiting her, for eradicating and dispersing Lucy's children. Even today, 'black' is the work done by her children, new slaves of the globalized times, who have chained themselves to sweat like slaves in some cold cement forest, save those who die on the voyage, who are swallowed up by what we used to call 'our sea,' but which is now 'their sea,' the Mediterranean, the sea of the dead. There's only one satisfaction left to Mother Africa: keeping her treasures locked in her own viscera, treasures like that black liquid gold for which men enslaved her and on whose fumes we now all asphyxiate ourselves."

Those were the black thoughts that assailed me that night, that first meeting with Jerry.

The next day, I listened to Jerry at an event organized to raise awareness. He really had the gift of speech; people were hanging on his every word. He talked about himself, his journey, our common homeland, his dreams, and most of all his hope for a future, the future Nelson Mandela projected. It's funny now to think that I had to come to Italy to discover the things I now know about him. Jerry alternated details about his childhood in the Transkei with anecdotes about the life of the *kaross*-wearing[7] Xhosa people in the *kraals*[8] in the veld. He described the round huts like beehives, with walls of banco, the straw roof supported by a central pillar. He told about stick fighting and described life in the village where practically only women and children lived because most men went to work on the big farms or in the mines. Some only returned twice a year to see their families and plow the fields. He also talked about the apartheid laws, the permits, the run-ins with the police, and life in the townships.

Jerry talked and talked, and then suddenly, furrowing his brow, looked lost in his recollections, as if he were trying to hold back a painful sigh of memory. I thought of the townships of Durban: Richmond Farm, KwaMashu, Lindelani, Ntuzuma, which, out of fear, I'd never seen, had always ignored. He told of the days when the *imbongi* told the stories and the old men explained the meaning of *ubuntu* and the dangers of its absence. "*Ubuntu ungamntu ngabanye abantu*" is a Xhosa proverb, "A person is a person through other persons," or in other words, we exist only through and for others. Respect, mutual help, and acceptance of others are sacred values for cultural intermingling.

When a bearded young man asked if this kind of intermingling wasn't just a utopian dream, Jerry showed that Mandela's vision is precisely that, a country of rainbow colors, a country that must reconcile with itself. "To live together, Blacks and Whites," he said, "we need to meet each other, to look each other in the eye, to have a dialogue that moves beyond our prejudices, with our differences and not despite our differences. To live together," he said, "we must move beyond our differences."

---

7   A rug or blanket of sewn animal skins, formerly worn as a garment by Xhosa people.

8   From Afrikaans, a cattle pen and a South African gated village.

To my embarrassment, he called me up to the head conference table and asked the audience, "Tell me, what differences are there between Sandra and me?"

And everyone in the crowd answered, "You're thinner than she is."

"You have a mustache, she does not."

"Fortunately for her!" Scattered laughter.

"You're a man and she's a woman."

"How insightful!"

Confronting the silence that followed, "What else? The most obvious thing . . . no one dares to say it?"

"She's white and you're black."

"Yes, but what else?"

"You wear glasses, she doesn't."

"Your hair is curly, hers is straight."

"Like spaghetti!" More laughter.

"She's blonde, and you have black hair."

"You have black eyes, she has blue eyes."

"You're dressed differently!"

"I haven't started wearing skirts yet! Well, okay, that's enough!"

When I made a move to return to my seat, he stopped me, "But I haven't finished our experiment! Now look at us closely and tell me what we have in common."

Silence.

"You both speak Italian."

"Yes."

More silence.

"You're both human beings!"

"Fantastic! What else?"

A longer silence.

"You both have two ears!"

"Yes! And a head, a nose, two legs, two arms, two feet as befits any human being! So, I think we can automatically include all these details in the definition of 'human being,' okay? So, anything else in common?"

A super long silence.

Another silence, squared. An awkward silence.

"Can you see that you had no difficulty in finding our differences, quite the contrary! But the question becomes more difficult when you're asked to look for what we have in common. Not because we have so much less in common, but simply because, unlike the differences, our similarities aren't obvious and aren't clearly visible. Our differences are visible to everyone and that's a good thing, but what we have in common is not as visible. Our bad habit of looking at people's differences, of judging others on the basis of appearances alone, has brought us to value only the external, and on that superficiality we have built the apartheid system. Looking at Sandra and me from the outside, none of you thought that we could have anything in common. You couldn't imagine, for example, that Sandra and I are both South Africans!"

"Ooh!"

"Yes, and yes again! Who would have said so? Not only are we from the same country but maybe we share the same dreams, the same faith, the same plans for the future of our children. Maybe we read the same books, or listen to the same music, or are fans of the same team, or fanatically follow the same political ideology! It's just possible that for the more important things in our lives that go beyond our appearances and whose skin has more or less melanin, to those things people don't see in the deepest part of our beings, perhaps there Sandra and I have more in common than she has with her own sister or others of her skin color.

"And yet out there, in our distant country, others have decided not to give us the opportunity to meet, to know each other, to have a real dialogue, and to learn to respect each other, to live side-by-side. We continue to nurture our prejudices and preconceptions due to ridiculous generalizations and even more, a mental laziness that leads us to label everything and judge others simplistically and banally by their exterior. Blacks, for example, think that Whites stink of garlic and don't wash."

As he said this Jerry turned to me with a slight knowing smile. "And some say that Black people have a strong odor." He continued, "And yet out there, in our far-off land, others have deprived and have continued for over twenty years to deprive a certain man of his freedom.

This man was robbed of one of the most precious commodities on this earth: time. Every day we all abuse this precious property belonging to others, by not keeping an appointment, for example, without realizing that it is one of those things that we can never give back. More than twenty years is more than two hundred and forty months, more than seven thousand days that no one, nothing can ever give back. This man is Nelson Mandela."

A long roar of applause greeted this name, and strangely enough, I too was applauding. I had goosebumps. Jerry stood up to embrace me, red-faced as I was with a revelation that was opening up new horizons before me. I had a furtive, wicked thought that was meant to be good. Fortunately, I was careful not to voice it, but I confess that while listening to Jerry, I'd been thinking that he was basically what at home we call a "coconut," black on the outside but white on the inside. That thought made me blush, knowing we still have a long way to go before achieving Mandela's dream.

Jerry left me that evening with a Xhosa greeting: "Goodbye, Sandra, Salakakuhle!"[9]

"Good luck, Jerry. Yangaungaphumelela!"[10]

Little did I know then that I would never see him again.

When I got back home, I joined the United Democratic Front, which united anti-apartheid groups, unions, the church, and students in protest, despite the bans. We all wanted two things: the release of Nelson Mandela and the end of apartheid.

Finally, my eyes were opened and I understood so much; certainly, not all my fears had left me. I was convinced that our future could only come through power-sharing, through free elections after Nelson Mandela's release: one man, one vote. But my brain wondered, given the law of numbers: would we not run the risk of moving from the dictatorship of a minority to that of a majority? How will the ANC[11]

---

9   From Xhosa, goodbye. Also written as "Sala Kakuhle."

10   From Xhosa, good luck. Also written as "Yangaunga Phumelela," "yanguanga" literally means "that you can join" and "phumelela" meaning "success" or "prosperity."

11   African National Congress, founded 1923, worked to end apartheid through the 1940s and 1950s, but was banned by the South African

behave with its thousand souls and all the ambitions frustrated for so many years? How would we manage to live together in peace, with the Whites fearing revenge and the Blacks holding grudges? How do we forgive and be forgiven?

I had so many questions I couldn't find answers to and I convinced myself that Jerry, who had opened my eyes, could have suggested possible solutions.

I looked forward to our reunion, for another chance to talk through so many of these things, to ask many questions. For the chance to thank him, and to figure out how to build a future.

It wasn't until I returned to Italy that I learned that Jerry had been murdered, murdered one night in August in an abandoned shack on the outskirts of Caserta, where he lived in deprivation, picking tomatoes, suffering the condition of an illegal immigrant, among those who never received the official political refugee status. In those days a wave of anger towards non-EU citizens had risen throughout Italy, a wave of madness, vile and reactionary. Fear took hold of the inhabitants of the countryside and the neighboring towns. First they collected signatures, then they marched against immigrants, and finally they attempted to lynch "the Blacks."

For them, the Xhosa proverb "Unyawo-alunampumlo"[12] was meaningless. "Unyawo-alunampumlo" evokes the fragility of exiles and reminds us of the moral obligation of each individual to offer help and defense to anyone who is far from home and lost among strangers.

So it was that one evening in August, two local men, two thugs, ran into the shacks where Jerry and his friends were resting and began their pillaging, taking what little savings those "outsiders" had earned that summer. Many of them, terrified, quickly gave up their money; others, like Jerry, had tried to reason with them. Why should they be robbed, in an instant, of the fruit of a whole month's work? He tried. Jerry and his friends opposed the arrogance of it all. So, Jerry stood

---

government from 1960 to 1990. Nelson Mandela was president of the ANC, which has since become the ruling party in South Africa.

12   The Xhosa proverb literally means "a foot has no nose." It is understood to mean "no one can detect what trouble may lie ahead of him, what life may hold for him."

in front of the guns, trying to understand . . . but all he got were four deadly slugs in the stomach. Others were injured, quickly rescued, and taken to the hospital, but for Jerry, it was too late.

Jerry's assassination marked a moment of great tension, and his death jolted the Italian conscience into giving more room for the values of tolerance and solidarity.

Only six months after Jerry's murder, on February 11, 1990, President De Klerk lifted the ban on the ANC, and Nelson Mandela was released, after twenty-seven years in prison. The bitterness of Jerry's tragic fate is somehow softened by the knowledge today that his sacrifice was not in vain, that he made it possible to change so many things in Italy from the laws to the living conditions of immigrants.

"Jerry had a dream . . . a world without hatred and racism, a world of tolerance and peace, of freedom and solidarity. A world where man is worth more than anything else, where his freedom is sacred, his dignity respected, his rights recognized. It was for those things that Jerry lived, hoped, and fought. With him, he carried the memory of his country oppressed by apartheid, the pain of his father and daughter massacred. Jerry is dead, killed by two criminals . . . Now Jerry's dream belongs to all men, white and black, who fight for a society free of racism and hatred, a tolerant and united society, where the individual and collective rights of all men and all peoples of the earth are recognized." Amongst some of Italy's highest authorities, one of Jerry's friends delivered these words at his funeral.

Jerry Essan Masslo escaped from South Africa to seek a better life in Italy and he died there.

ABOUT THE AUTHOR

Born in Togo in 1954, KOSSI AMÉKOWOYOA KOMLA-EBRI is a medical surgeon who lives near Como. His publications include the novel *Neyla* (Madison FDU Press, 2004), winner of the Premio Prato CittAperta 2019, and collections of short stories, tales, and anecdotes including *Imbarazzismi* (translated into English as *EmbarRACEments*, Bordighera Press, 2019). He is the winner of the 2005 Premio Mare Nostrum for Literature and Premio Graphein by Società di Pedagogia e Didattica della Scrittura in 2009.

ABOUT THE TRANSLATOR

MARIE ORTON is Professor of Italian at Brigham Young University. Her English translation of Kossi Komla-Ebri's *Imbarazzismi* and *Nuovi imbarazzismi* was published as *EmbaRACEments: Daily Embarrassments in Black and White . . . and Color* in 2019. She recently co-edited the volume *Contemporary Italian Diversity in Critical and Fictional Narratives* (Farleigh Dickinson UP, 2021) with Graziella Parati and Ron Kubati. She is currently researching the intersections of migration and constructed cultural memory in the medium of museums.

CROSSINGS

An Intersection of Cultures

Crossings is dedicated to the publication of Italian language literature and translations from Italian to English.

Rodolfo Di Biasio. *Wayfarers Four*. Translated by Justin Vitello. 1998. ISBN 1-88419-17-9. Vol 1.

Isabella Morra. *Canzoniere: A Bilingual Edition*. Translated by Irene Musillo Mitchell. 1998. ISBN 1-88419-18-6. Vol 2.

Nevio Spadone. *Lus*. Translated by Teresa Picarazzi. 1999. ISBN 1-88419-22-4. Vol 3.

Flavia Pankiewicz. *American Eclipses*. Translated by Peter Carravetta. Introduction by Joseph Tusiani. 1999. ISBN 1-88419-23-2. Vol 4.

Dacia Maraini. *Stowaway on Board*. Translated by Giovanna Bellesia and Victoria Offredi Poletto. 2000. ISBN 1-88419-24-0. Vol 5.

Walter Valeri, editor. *Franca Rame: Woman on Stage*. 2000. ISBN 1-88419-25-9. Vol 6.

Carmine Biagio Iannace. *The Discovery of America*. Translated by William Boelhower. 2000. ISBN 1-88419-26-7. Vol 7.

Romeo Musa da Calice. *Luna sul salice*. Translated by Adelia V. Williams. 2000. ISBN 1-88419-39-9. Vol 8.

Marco Paolini & Gabriele Vacis. *The Story of Vajont*. Translated by Thomas Simpson. 2000. ISBN 1-88419-41-0. Vol 9.

Silvio Ramat. *Sharing A Trip: Selected Poems*. Translated by Emanuel di Pasquale. 2001. ISBN 1-88419-43-7. Vol 10.

Raffaello Baldini. *Page Proof*. Edited by Daniele Benati. Translated by Adria Bernardi. 2001. ISBN 1-88419-47-X. Vol 11.

Maura Del Serra. *Infinite Present*. Translated by Emanuel di Pasquale and Michael Palma. 2002. ISBN 1-88419-52-6. Vol 12.

Dino Campana. *Canti Orfici*. Translated and Notes by Luigi Bonaffini. 2003. ISBN 1-88419-56-9. Vol 13.

Roberto Bertoldo. *The Calvary of the Cranes*. Translated by Emanuel di Pasquale. 2003. ISBN 1-88419-59-3. Vol 14.

Paolo Ruffilli. *Like It or Not*. Translated by Ruth Feldman and James Laughlin. 2007. ISBN 1-88419-75-5. Vol 15.

Giuseppe Bonaviri. *Saracen Tales*. Translated Barbara De Marco. 2006. ISBN 1-88419-76-3. Vol 16.

Leonilde Frieri Ruberto. *Such Is Life*. Translated Laura Ruberto. Introduction by Ilaria Serra. 2010. ISBN 978-1-59954-004-7. Vol 17.

Gina Lagorio. *Tosca the Cat Lady*. Translated by Martha King. 2009. ISBN 978-1-59954-002-3. Vol 18.

Marco Martinelli. *Rumore di acque*. Translated and edited by Thomas Simpson. 2014. ISBN 978-1-59954-066-5. Vol 19.

Emanuele Pettener. *A Season in Florida*. Translated by Thomas De Angelis. 2014. ISBN 978-1-59954-052-2. Vol 20.

Angelo Spina. *Il cucchiaio trafugato*. 2017. ISBN 978-1-59954-112-9. Vol 21.

Michela Zanarella. *Meditations in the Feminine*. Translated by Leanne Hoppe. 2017. ISBN 978-1-59954-110-5. Vol 22.

Francesco "Kento" Carlo. *Resistenza Rap*. Translated by Emma Gainsforth and Siân Gibby. 2017. ISBN 978-1-59954-112-9. Vol 23.

Kossi Komla-Ebri. *EMBAR-RACE-MENTS*. Translated by Marie Orton. 2019. ISBN 978-1-59954-124-2. Vol 24.

Angelo Spina. *Immagina la prossima mossa*. 2019. ISBN 978-1-59954-153-2. Vol 25.

Luigi Lo Cascio. *Othello*. Translated by Gloria Pastorino. 2020. ISBN 978-1-59954-158-7. Vol 26.

Sante Candeloro. *Puzzle*. Translated by Fred L. Gardaphe. 2020. ISBN 978-1-59954-165-5. Vol 27.

Amerigo Ruggiero. *Italians in America*. Translated by Mark Pietralunga. 2020. ISBN 978-1-59954-169-3. Vol 28.

Giuseppe Prezzolini. *The Transplants*. Translated by Fabio Girelli Carasi. 2021. ISBN 978-1-59954-137-2. Vol 29.

Silvana La Spina. *Penelope*. Translated by Anna Chiafele and Lisa Pike. 2021. ISBN 978-1-59954-172-3. Vol 30.

Marino Magliani. *A Window to Zeewijk*. Translated by Zachary Scalzo. 2021. ISBN 978-1-59954-178-5. Vol 31.

Alain Elkann. *Anita*. Translated by K.E. Bättig von Wittelsbach. 2021. ISBN 978-1-59954-170-9. Vol 32.

Luigi Fontanella. *The God of New York*. Translated by Siân E. Gibby. 2022. ISBN 978-1-59954-177-8. Vol 33.

www.ingramcontent.com/pod-product-compliance
Lightning Source LLC
Chambersburg PA
CBHW020024030726
47499CB00007B/2264